MODELS AND LOVERS
BY
Johnny Ray
Copyright © 2012
PUBLISHED BY
SIR JOHN PUBLISHING

ALL RIGHTS ARE HEREBY
RESERVED BY JOHNNY RAY

DEDICATIONS

This work is dedicated to my wife and best friend Natasha Ray, who encouraged me daily to keep working to make this book the best ever.

I want to thank my friends with TARA, the Tampa Bay Chapter of the Romance Writers of America, who have given me so much support in my writing.

Also, where would any writer be without a great editor? My editor for this book, James lee VunKannon worked hard to help me polish this book.

Finally, I want to thank all of my beta readers, reviewers, and most importantly, my fans for their continued support.

Johnny Ray is an award winning novelist who won the Royal Palm literary award for best thriller and is quickly making a name for himself as the master of the romantic thriller. He loves social interaction with his readers and can be found on

Twitter
 www.twitter.com/sirjohn_writer

Facebook
www.facebook.com/authorjohnnyray.

He can also be reached by e-mailing at
sirjohnnyray@gmail.com

Or you can just follow him on his blog at
 www.sirjohn.us
 for updates and future releases.

Johnny Ray's novels

A WAR HERO RETURNS
Published by Sir John Publishing in 2013

JOHN RAIN–THE HAWAIIAN AFFAIR
Published by AMAZON DIGITAL in 2013

STALKING LOVE
Published by Sir John Publishing in 2013

LITERARY AGENT–BEWARE
Published by Sir John Publishing in 2012

SCANDAL–THE DEATH OF A LEGACY
Published by Sir John Publishing in 2012

DRONES
Published by Sir John Publishing in 2013

HER HONOR'S BODYGUARD
Published by Sir John Publishing in 2012

FOR LOVE AND VENGEANCE
Published by Sir John Publishing in 2012

THE SALSA CONNECTION
Published by Sir John Publishing in 2012

THE JOURNEY TO WHITESTONE
Published by Sir John Publishing in 2012

Chapter 1

Balarie Danson's excited squeal shattered the eerie silence as she flipped the switch to her new office. Suddenly embarrassed by the scream of overflowing joy, she glanced around. She assumed, or at least hoped, no one else worked this late.

Finally, she had landed the chance to prove to the fashion world what she could do. After so many years of dedication and struggling to get by, the sweet rewards of her success appeared to be so close that she could almost taste it.

She raced around her desk and dove into the dark brown chair on the other side, inhaling its leathery aroma. While nicely furnished with paintings and coordinated artwork, the space still needed her personal touch, which was why she had decided to work late with no one else around to bother her.

Balarie glanced at the boxes which contained her personal items such as some awards and photos of her working with various models and designers. While earlier in her career she had initially obtained some modeling work for herself, she had become a master at helping her modeling friends find work, which eventually caught the agency's attention. Her move from a modeling career to handling other models with one of the best modeling agencies in New York City may have surprised many people, but none more than herself.

After walking toward the boxes, she stopped, as the presence of someone standing in her office doorway startled her. She swirled to confront the intruder—her new boss and the owner of the agency bearing his name. "Mr. Conseco! I didn't know you were here."

Thomas Conseco didn't smile as he studied her. He looked taller than earlier. Being slightly over six feet herself, Balarie seldom looked up at many guys, especially in the four inch heels she often wore. "I heard someone yell. Was that you?"

That's embarrassing. She decided to be honest. "I'm excited about working here. Sorry, I thought I was alone."

"Good." The features of his face shifted into the signature smile she remembered from earlier. "I hope your enthusiasm will last after you see how demanding this work can be. And by the way, you can call me Tommy."

"Yes, sir. I mean, Tommy. I hope its okay I came in tonight to get my office ready."

"This isn't a bad idea. We have a staff meeting at nine tomorrow, and where I'll be introducing you." As he stared over the top of his light rose-colored sunglasses, she wondered why he even wore them at night.

"I'll be there. I want to get into my role here as fast as possible."

"You're going to have your hands full handling some of the male models we represent. Many bookers don't like working with them. My best advice to you is to find work for your top models before they leave us. You'll never have a better time to make an impression than now."

"Thanks. I plan to start interviewing all of them as soon as possible. Your agency has a fantastic reputation, and I want to uphold the name as best I can."

The fact he talked to her openly made her feel at ease, but the constant stares confused her. Was he checking her out? She knew she hadn't dressed in office clothes for the night, but she had never expected to see anyone, especially the owner at this late hour.

Tommy, on the other hand, dressed as if he would be the main attraction on a fashion runway. His hair, a dark-brown containing streaks of blond running through it looked gorgeous! The style was a mixture of a professional business man and artistic flare, obviously the creation of a world-class stylist. While many guys showed signs of a five o'clock shadow on their face, Tommy remained clean and neat, showcasing his high cheek bones and rugged jaw lines, the perfect requirements of a male model. At the distance apart from him she couldn't tell the true color of his eyes but they were light colored and perhaps blue. She suddenly wondered if he had ever modeled himself.

"I certainly hope you remember our reputation is on the line every day. I know this is after hours, but any time you come to the agency be sure to dress appropriately. Many times at night we have clients dropping by to check on a shooting. And as you know, there are emergencies that can come up at anytime which have to be handled."

She knew his comments were a polite way to tell her not to dress like this again. She took the message to heart as she started to apologize.

He raised his hand to stop her. "I think that will be all. Good luck on getting set up tonight and on your first appearance tomorrow." As he turned to leave, she studied his suit. She wished she could name the designer, but couldn't. Whoever it was had tailored him perfectly by highlighting his muscular body underneath the suit.

"Thanks, I'm not going to be here long. I hope to make it to the gym tonight. Thank you for the warning about clients coming by late at night. I'll remember it."

Tommy turned to face Balarie once more. "It's a little late to work out, but it is better than never. I'll see to it you receive an invitation to join my sports club." He paused. "You have a chance to make a name for yourself here. If you do, you'll also be a large help to our Paris and Milan office. I know you'll love to see them soon."

Panic swept through her. Going to Paris or Milan was impossible! She had made it through the first thirty years of her life without riding on a plane and had no intention of ever boarding one. Fearing this could cost her this dream job, she decided to hide the fact. Later, much later, she would tell him and hope for the best. She needed to respond, but how?

"Before I leave, let me give you one piece of advice the previous owner of this agency gave me when he sold it to me fifteen years ago." His perfect white teeth glistened as he stepped deeper inside her office. He was either genetically gifted, or they were capped. He raised his fingers in a pyramid in front of his face before he continued. She understood body language enough to recognize the obvious signs of superiority but she expected such from him.

She nodded her head in appreciation of his advice, wondering exactly what he planned to say.

"He told me the number one piece of advice I needed to stick with involved screwing anyone involved with the agency. This is why I enforce a strict rule against it. I'm sure you remember signing a copy of our policy and procedure manual when you passed through personnel."

"Yes and that makes sense to me."

"It's much harder than you can imagine, but it becomes easier after you've firmly established your name and professionalism."

"I don't think you have anything to worry about. I don't date, and I work almost all of the time. My one vice is my physical training. I have to have my work outs."

"Good, I see we share one interest. Since you're going to be handling the men here, it would be good for you to make contacts with many gyms around the city. You'll receive a complete list of breakdowns tomorrow on your desk, but you won't have long to study the information before the meeting."

"Thanks, I'll do my best."

"Your best is good, but results will help you keep your job."

She didn't expect him to be so brutally open on her first work day but knew he spoke the truth. Her job as a booker was to find jobs. She could make one hundred thousand dollars or she could make five hundred thousand. Her income all depended on how many quality bookings she landed. She felt glad the manager handled the careers of the models, leaving her to concentrate on sales.

As he turned to leave, she noticed his shoes. He wore Cuban type heels with the heels themselves made of some sort of an antique looking silver metal. The extra two to three inches was what added to his height.

As she raised her stare back to his face, he tilted his head to one side. "I see you noticed my shoes. These are a gift from Tony Marcello. He knows how much I love to dance tango, and he designed these for me."

Balarie walked closer. "I hate to stare, but may I see them again?"

Tommy bent his knee slightly and lifted

the material on his pants to reveal the shoes. As she dropped to one knee to look closer at the elaborate details of a silver and gold imprinted sun radiating in several directions, the quality of the workmanship mesmerized her. "Okay, like wow, this is one designer you have to introduce me to."

Tommy allowed the bottom hem which flared slightly to fall to the floor. "That you can count on, he'll become one of our major clients soon. He has a flair for design which outpaces many expert shoe designers."

As Balarie stood, she looked into his ocean-blue eyes, a color she'd suspected earlier. His scent, perhaps a British Creed, floated toward her. She remembered avoiding many men over the last several years. This time she wondered if he really kept his word of avoiding sex with everyone in the modeling world. His vibes certainly didn't convey his words. "I'll admit to one more vice. I'm crazy about shoes. Buying the latest is where I spend most of my money."

"I see. When words circulates that you do, expect to receive many shoes from designers who will be sending you their . . . latest. I'll expect you to keep a level head in all of this."

"I can return them if—."

"What for? Enjoy it." He glanced around the office. "I'll check back on you later and see what you did here." He left as he pulled the door closed behind him. Was this his way of making sure no one else saw her in her fatigues?

Since he had built this modeling agency into a power house in the modeling industry he had to be one smart dedicated guy. She needed to learn everything she could from him if she ever hoped to own her own agency later. She knew she had just gotten her foot in the door, but it was a good foot. She needed to learn the names of all of the top clients and how to satisfy their needs.

She turned toward the boxes she had delivered which would add her distinct look to the room, but she knew it would be dismal compared to the other seasoned bookers in the agency. She would use what she had. Since Tommy said he would be coming back to see what she did to the room, she needed to make a call soon to another friend, an interior decorator.

Chapter 2

Balarie rushed into her office carrying her portfolio and much needed hot morning coffee. Her office, unfortunately, looked exactly as she had left it a few hours ago. Damn, she hoped this morning she would have the breakdowns highlighting what the buyers would be looking for, the one Tommy promised the night before. With so many models under contract, she hadn't memorized many of the names yet. She continued to flip through many of the head shots and picked out some she thought would be the best to work with. She needed to meet as many of their models as possible.

She turned on her computer and studied the layout of the company's site. The girl she replaced had ventured off on her own and left many accounts neglected. Some of the models would naturally follow her, but not many.

It was decision time. Should she explore around the office, or wait until Tommy made her formal introduction in an hour?

And was Tommy a name she could use openly, or only in private? She expected she would have to say a few words after being introduced. Except for Tommy and the girl in personnel, she hadn't met anyone else with the agency.

Her phone rang. She knew that represented her life line and expected to be on it most of the time. "Hello, this is Balarie."

"Hi, have you heard anything yet?" Joseph, her best friend in the city, acted anxious, but she couldn't blame him since he wanted a job working with her. Balarie knew she needed an assistant and Joe would be perfect.

"I just started here and I'll need some time. Don't worry. I'll call you soon."

"Cool. I hope to hear from you soon."

She heard a small knock on the door as she replaced the phone. A guy, obviously from their mail room walked over to her. "I have a package for you."

"Thanks." She accepted what she thought looked like the breakdowns and started studying what buyers were looking for. Landing a major slick magazine account or advertising firm would be extraordinary, however she knew that would take some time.

Thirty minutes later she heard the outer

office coming alive with people rushing by her personal space. Hectic conversations erupted as people passed along the hallway leading to the conference room.

One girl stopped to knock on her door. "You must be the new girl."

"Yes, I'm Balarie."

"I know. I heard your name. You need to hurry."

"Why? We still have thirty minutes."

A look of shock passed her face. "My name's Olivia, Mr. Conseco's assistant. We need to talk soon. I have the agenda for the meeting on the conference table. He expects everyone to read and know what's going on before the meeting starts." Olivia glanced out the door. Her outfit highlighted her sculptured body like a glove. With large muscles for a girl, she looked more like a physical trainer than a professional secretary. The spiked hair Balarie could live with if Olivia worked the runway side of the agency, but as a professional secretary to the owner. . . .

Not knowing what to expect, Balarie retrieved her files and carried her portfolio with her. She felt good in her own power suit. As a booker she assumed the agency required her to look professional. Her days of modeling herself were over. The fear of flying had ended all hope of making it as a model.

As Balarie walked into the conference room, she watched twelve nervous people concentrating on the papers in front of them. No one raised a head to say hello. The large masculine, executive chair at the head of the table left no doubt who would be sitting there. The place of honor was the only chair with armrests. At the far end of the table she saw one open seat. It must be hers.

Balarie studied the projection screen directly behind her. She had been given the worst seat in the room if they showed a presentation she needed to watch. She slid into her seat and glanced around the room.

An older man glanced in her direction briefly before checking his watch. His quick appraisal left her cold as he refocused on the papers. Okay, she got the message. She opened the papers in front of her.

Olivia rushed in again. "He's on his way. I hope everyone's prepared."

After meeting Tommy last night, she couldn't understand why everyone acted so nervous about him coming. She saw nothing too important in the agenda. It looked like normal progress reports to her.

The side door swung open and Tommy walked over to his seat without recognizing anyone. "I know I'm a few minutes early, but we need to get started. We have a busy day planned."

Nervous glances turned to brilliant smiles. Okay, this looked better. "I assume everyone had time to read the agenda this morning, but before we begin, I want to introduce a new team player. This is Balarie Danson, who will be joining us as a booker and specializing in helping our male models secure some better paying jobs."

Balarie offered a small wave as the attention focused on her.

"She has some modeling experience, although limited. But, she has managed to meet the right people while looking for work."

The elder gentleman next to her spoke in a deep Brooklyn accent. "So . . . she has never worked for an agency before."

"That would be correct. I thought it would be good to try someone new without all of the baggage many bookers have with the industry. We all know male models don't make as much as their female counter parts. I think by having her concentrate on just men she'll gain a whole new focus on how to book them. This might also help us in recruiting if she can land some major accounts for us. We'll all be watching her closely."

There was nothing like feeling the

pressure from day one. She felt her palms sweating as she watched the constant stares.

"But rather than hearing it from me, Balarie, tell us a little about you and what you hope to do here."

She took a deep breath as she felt the intense scrutiny tightening around her. "Yes . . . as Mr. Conseco mentioned, I'm new at booking models for an agency, but I had some success in finding work for other models I knew. I've met some of the buyers in New York, and I'll work hard on the others."

A tall girl with model qualities across from her spoke next. "Are you planning on doing any modeling yourself?"

"While I would love to do some modeling, I don't think this job will allow me any time to model." Balarie shook her hair slightly in case some of the curls dangled out of place.

"You have some good qualities. Do you still have a promo card with you?"

"I do, but wasn't planning on using it other than as an example of what might be needed."

"I would like to see it. One thing you have to remember is that managing the career of the models, male or female is for the manager, and your job is to find work and take care of the details in making it go as smoothly as possible. Sometimes it can be a fine line. Over-stepping is one thing which cost the booker you are replacing her job. I don't want to face the same problem again."

"I don't know much about her, but I assume I'll hear more soon. I know you're the manager that I'll be working with, and I do know the differences in the roles. I plan to keep up my part of the equation." Already a direct challenge. She dealt with her kind before. They were usually beauty queens spoiled by rich parents. "I'm very thankful for the opportunity here and hope I can do my part."

###

Tommy studied the reactions around the room. He knew hiring Balarie Danson, a midlist model, would cause some doubts, but he knew something they didn't. She had already caught the eye of Samantha Koppel, the buyer for several magazines which also included A MAN'S WORLD, one of the top male-centered magazines in the world. Exposure on this cover could ignite the careers of many of their models to greater things.

He studied Balarie's features. She had the height and the high jawbones of a professional model, but she lacked that the little something extra, one of those things he had a hard time explaining. She looked cute, damn cute, but didn't have the beautiful, mystic look of a supermodel that she needed to make it to the top tier. She had too much of the simple girl next door persona.

Her blonde hair reached her shoulders and curled too much. If it occurred naturally, she needed to see about having it relaxed.

If she helped it along, she needed better advice. Still, he thought, it added a certain charm to her face. Her breasts looked firm, and hopefully natural, but from photos of her that he had reviewed earlier, she had a small, flat butt. Not a bad thing for the runway, but for fashion it hurt her chances tremendously.

"Let me introduce the rest of the staff to you." He paused for a second and glanced at his newest Swiss watch, designed by his friend at Lancer. "Better yet, I'll let everyone introduce yourself as you give your report. I trust you've studied the files. These numbers suck. I don't want finger pointing, but I do want to know why it looks like we have all been on vacation lately."

He motioned to the first person on his left. He knew what they would be saying before they started. It was always about the competition. No one admitted their own faults. Every model gave them problems and distinct headaches. He thought how it would be so refreshing to hear someone take the blame for a failure for once.

As the progression advanced around the table the attention turned to Balarie and halted. She remained still with an innocent but amusing smile. "You're next," he added.

Tommy watched her scramble to read the notes. With an arched eyebrow, she raised her head. "Today's my first day, so I'll apologize for not being prepared. I only saw this a few minutes ago."

"Since you have nothing to add to the meeting, I suggest you get to work and be prepared for the meeting next week." He studied the shock on her face, and the hurt he inflicted, but still, she was another worker, who appeared to be wasting his time. Perhaps he had made a mistake in hiring her. Only time would tell. He would have much more enjoyed giving her compliments. Should he make an exception and go out of his way to help her. Should he? She did offer a strange allure to his normal stiff defense. Maybe he was getting weak. Time would tell.

Balarie stood, but faced him directly.

"I'm not sure who prepared these notes, however whoever plans to go to the MacHenry exhibit later this afternoon will be in for a surprise. The designer is a no show, and I expect the attendance will be sparse. The time will be better spent attending a shoe show hosted by a

new guy from the garment district. While he's not known to many, his innovative style should attract several magazine writers and other designers not wanting to be left behind."

One girl giggled. "And does this new startup have money to spend on advertising?"

"Perhaps later . . . but two other possibilities exist. One, his small company could be absorbed by a larger one, or two, a good contact could be made with someone in the audience."

"It sounds like a shot in the dark to me."

Balarie shifted in her direction while still standing. "Or . . . it could be the shot heard around the world." She refocused her smile as if to give him a challenge. "I think you're right, I've a lot of work to do. So, if you'll excuse me, I'll get busy."

Spunky he liked, but a direct confrontation he never allowed. "Please do. I hope you make us all proud."

As he watched her walk away, the dress

draped her body perfectly as it flowed with her pace. Her work out regiment appeared very effective in sculpturing her body. While she looked physically fit, she still lacked the signature qualities of a supermodel. He assumed a size two. Her solid firm breasts, held in place with the low cut blouse, had highlighted her cleavage. He would have loved to give her a passing smile, but now with the others focused on his every move. Still, her skin radiated with a glow which made her hard to ignore.

As she left the room, he concentrated on one last thought. *Why had no one else told me about a shoe designer right under my nose? Should I make a surprise visit? Should I?*

Chapter 3

Balarie left the conference room confused. While she thought Conseco would have more of a team that pulled together on the same page, she never expected adversaries. At least she knew the rules now. She entered her office long enough to drop off her load and give her makeup a quick once over. With everyone in the meeting she had time to explore the agency which occupied three floors. Her office, stuck in the middle of the management section, had no windows, but that would change one day. For now she worked on the inside, but she needed help. She needed to make sure she developed a team of her own around her.

She retrieved a copy of her birth certificate that the girl in personnel had requested the day before. Balarie also needed to ask questions, but most importantly, she needed an assistant she could trust, and she knew Joseph would watch her back. She walked deliberately along the halls as many people stared at her. It felt funny watching many employees return a sheepish smile, while not knowing who she was.

Upon seeing Balarie, the girl in personnel acted surprised. "I thought you were in a meeting?"

"Since I didn't have a lot to offer, Mr. Conseco dismissed me from the group. I need to get up to speed as fast as possible and I was told I would have an assistant."

"You should have a temp arriving in a few minutes. We'll make arrangement for someone permanent in the next few days."

"I understand, but I've someone in mind and he can start today."

The girl dropped the papers she was sorting. "I would be glad to talk to anyone, but I think you know we have people wanting to intern here and work for almost nothing."

"The guy I have in mind isn't looking for major money now, but would love to have the opportunity. He's also highly efficient, which is what I need to have working for me."

"The best I can do is give him a temporary status until he's checked out and approved."

"Good, he'll be in shortly to see you. You can send the other girl home." Balarie reached for her cell as she added, "His name's Joseph but goes by Joe."

Balarie walked out as she waited for Joe to answer his phone. He would be an incredible asset. His gay lifestyle didn't bother her. This was strictly work related and Joe knew people, lots of people. No one could get her into parties like he could. She laughed at the remarks of paying him. His dad owned real estate all over the city, making him one of the richest men in New York City.

"Hello, I've been waiting on you to call me."

"I thought so. Come on over. I have you a temporary approval until they check you out. I also have the breakdown of what everyone's looking for and need to know how to contact them. We need to concentrate on the top ten targets."

"I'm on my way. We still have time to see the shoe show this afternoon, don't we?"

"I wouldn't miss it. Ciao." She snapped the phone shut.

Not wanting to be seen from the conference room, which had a glass front, she descended the stairs to the production area hosting shooting rooms available for some staff photographers. The stairways appeared cold and daunting, but it was a place she would know well since taking the elevator would always be out of the question. She had promised herself she would stay in condition and not allow her new job to ruin her health.

The rooms looked impressive, with many preset backdrops and multiple lighting sources available. Several younger guys studied her as she walked across the open area in the center of the floor. Finally, one photographer assistant approached her. "Are you one of the models we're supposed to shoot at ten?"

She extended him a hand. "No, I'm new here. My name's Balarie Danson, and I'll be booking some of the male models working for us."

"I heard we hired someone new who would be starting today. The guys will love working with you."

Balarie ignored the pass for now. "I'm sure they will, and especially if I can keep them busy making money. It's going to be fascinating watching you guys working. I want to meet our models and obtain updated photos of them as fast as we can."

"The closer you can describe the look you're looking for, the better we can accommodate you."

"Good. We need to create some super stars to get our name where it's supposed to be. I want the male models to speak volumes for us."

"You have a lofty goal, but remember that the girls here pay the bills."

"They have in the past, but I hope to make the males give them a run for their money."

Another guy walked over to them. His long, dark, wavy hair matched his dark but short beard. His mannerism placed him as the photographer in charge, as the assistant backed behind his alpha male presence. "I heard you talking. My name's Ethan. Welcome to my world."

Balarie remembered the name. He managed the photographic studio for the agency. While the bulk of his job included building comps and promotional cards for the models, he occasionally did shooting for clients. "I hope to interview many of the models over the next few days. I could use a quick tour if you have a minute."

"It will be my pleasure." He pointed to the different shooting areas. "I can have different moods established and the lighting balanced for almost any kind of scene. I don't know of many professional photographers in town with this nice of a set up."

She remembered seeing better, but allowed it to drop for now. The ceiling hung too low for one thing. It also seemed to be cramped for adequate space to work. One large shooting area might be better. She imagined they handled lots of shooting in the studio. In addition to the models they needed to promote, the agency also ran a school on another floor. The students paid for their own shooting. She could only imagine how much the agency made off of those dreams.

"When you shoot models, how do you accommodate everyone in such a small spot?"

"We have additional rooms for people to work. The makeup and hair styling people all have their own spaces while wardrobes are in another. When the model is in front of me, I want no distractions. It's my way of doing things."

"Okay, show me. I need to understand your procedure." She followed him from one room to the next where he did have it well thought out.

"Additionally, we do our own editing and printing here. Another girl does all of the digital alterations and Photoshop enhancements. Because we generate most of the outgoing mail, the mail room is at the end of this hallway."

"What about video productions?"

"It's in a different section. We don't have many singers we represent but we're prepared for it when we do with a separate sound room."

After thirty minutes of walking from one room to another she had a good idea of what they could do. "Thank you. I'm sure you'll see me in and out of here a lot in the near future."

"I look forward to it." Ethan leaned closer to her. "If you ever want personal shots, let me know also. I assume you still model some."

"What makes you think so?"

He leaned even closer and offered a million dollar smile that she had witness so many times before by other photographers. "The questions you asked, and the way you analyzed the setting is from the view point of a model instead of as a technician or manager."

"Yes, I've modeled before. The technical part is why we hire people like you."

"With that, I think we'll get along with each other great. I need to get ready for the morning shoots. Stop by later and watch us in action." He paused for a minute as if to send a special message she didn't completely understand, but assumed he intended it to be flirty. A boyfriend was one problem she definitely had no time for. She only had a short window to prove what she could do.

She had two more floors to visit. The next floor housed the modeling school. While not a part of her main job she needed to know what they provided and keep her eye out for possibilities. As she socialized, she would also be promoting the school, where she would also be earning commissions on all students she directed there.

After walking through the front door, she felt impressed immediately. Tommy played up the magical allure of the modeling industry very well, with several photos of him adorning the walls, and his striking images effectively branding the company.

As she walked closer to study one photo, a tall slim blonde with big breasts and high jaw bones walked over to her. "May I help you?"

Again, Balarie introduced herself and explored the school on the fly. She would return later, but had to move on for now. The main office containing the accounting and advertising departments worked on the next level. This functional styled office was designed to be efficient and far from glamorous. She met the office manager the day before. Gaining her help would be crucial. She needed to know which clients in their data base would be the best ones to hit first, and which ones could be expanded.

Thirty minutes later, Balarie knew her morning had disappeared, but she had completed the bases she needed to start with. Her phone rang. She saw Joe's name of the caller ID. "Are you here yet?"

"Yes, I'm in your office. We have some major work to do here. Have you seen where they want me to work?"

"Sorry, there's not much I can do about this area now." She knew Joe and he would have the image changed by tomorrow, even if it meant spending his own money to do so.

"Oh, I'm not bitching, and you know I'll take care of it."

"I'm on my way up." She looked forward to the afternoon shoe show, but needed to study her files on the models she must work with also. Memorizing them would be a lot to accomplish in a few hours.

Chapter 4

Balarie rushed toward her office, hoping the rest of her files she ordered would be waiting on her. After walking through the door, she collided with Tommy who was leaving her office. "Sorry, I didn't see you, Mr. Conseco." The close proximity froze her thoughts. *Why did he come to check up on me?* He had treated her so cold in the meeting to be staring so intently at her now.

"No, it's my fault." He backed slightly from her. "The shoe show you mentioned at the meeting intrigued me. I came by to find out where it was being held. I assume you'll be heading to it shortly."

"I don't have a lot of time, but hope to make a showing." Balarie saw Joe standing behind Tommy. "I assume you met my assistant."

"Yes, he gave me the information I needed and I think I might have met his parents a time or two." Tommy turned to face her again. "It's good to see someone taking charge so quickly, but be careful since you have many others gunning for your job. I don't mean on the staff here, but in the fashion world in this city and around the world. Working here will make you a target."

"I know how competitive it is and I think I can hold my own."

"Bring in some accounts and then we'll see. Also, try not to lose the ones you're given." Tommy winked while maintaining a solemn face, sending a mixed message to her before he turned and walked away.

She watched people scatter in the outer offices as he walked by. She recognized the heavy armor around his emotions. The modeling agency must have made him like this. While parts of him she knew she needed to mold herself after, the other parts she hoped she never would.

After he disappeared, she turned to Joe. "We don't have much time. I need to like totally memorize the models I'm responsible for and who they have worked for recently. Those relationships have to be cemented as we go to work on finding new bookings. Let's start with the top dozen or so and expand from there. See if you can arrange a meeting with the models starting tomorrow morning and I'll work on calling their last jobs. I need to make

appearance around town to let everyone

know we're here to handle their needs."

"I guess that means working through lunch, huh?"

"You got it. But don't worry. We'll have some fun along the way." Whatever it took for her to establish herself she would do. But, she also felt like enjoying life was important. Her southern upbringing and values would never disappear.

###

While Tommy acted like he had never heard of the shoe designer before, he had. This show, however, caught him off guard. If Balarie was correct, others would be in attendance that he knew. His passion for shoes never ended. He knew of no other man in the city with over five hundred pairs. Many had been designed for him and some represented collectables, worn by actors during movies or famous people of some sort.

The style he took pride in were dancing shoes worn by the men in Argentina. He also loved the Spanish dancers. The sound on the floor of a good shoe said it all. Those firm solid steps clicked the beats of the rhythm better than any drummer could dream of.

He knew he might run into Balarie or her assistant while attending, but so be it. His presence wouldn't go unnoticed. There were no tickets to buy. The show was cast in the back of the shop where Aaron Chinell designed and sold his shoes. He created special limited edition runs, perfect for the select people who could afford his designs. If he did manage to form a partnership with a major player who could mass produce them, he could become a major client overnight.

As Tommy approached the staged area, he saw Balarie on the front row where she was taking notes. He walked in her direction as he surveyed the people around her. He saw no one he knew.

After approaching to within about ten feet, Balarie glanced toward him and smiled before handing a file to Joe. "Wow, it's good to see you here. Since you asked for the address and time from Joe, I thought you might make it. We saved a seat for you."

"You'll learn soon enough that I have a serious weakness for shoes. So tell me what you've learned about this Aaron Chinell."

"His shoes aren't cheap, but because he has limited production capabilities, his name's not too well known. While he has fought

mass production for most of his career, he's considering an offer which will make him wealthy and able to expand his business. I heard he hasn't made his mind up yet. There will be an after party, and this is where I hope to meet some other people attending."

"I wish I could stay for it, but I need to get back to the office."

"I understand."

As the show began, Tommy glanced across the room. Much like faces drifting out of the dark, he recognized several of his competitors from other agencies lurking closer. He also noted several magazine editors venturing along the edges. While they practiced the good sense of mingling unnoticed with the crowd, he sat in front of everyone, and fully on display. As flashes came from the fringes of the runway, he recognized several of the paparazzi from before and he knew his photo would appear somewhere tomorrow. It usually did. Being caught out with a different woman would start new speculations. The tabloids always wanted to nail him to an affair. Hell, let them say what they want. They would never know the truth. His personal life would always be protected. But, then again, what personal life?

Forty-five minutes later the show ended and the designer walked on stage. He waved at several people in the stands who were apparently avid fans of his and who had purchased his shoes before. Tommy made many mental notes and would order a few pairs. His assistant would handle it for him tomorrow. For now, he needed to leave. He turned to Balarie and cupped a hand to be heard over the crowd disbursing around him. "Thanks for letting me know of this. You have a crowd here you need to work. Good luck. By the way, I'm having a party tomorrow night at my place. I want you to meet some more people. If you think of any other people in the industry we need to entertain, please feel free to invite them. I use this as a marketing tool for the company, and you should avail yourself of the opportunity."

"Thank you. I'll be there."

Tommy adjusted in his seat as more flashes centered in on him. He could only imagine how the cupped hand would add to the speculation. He must leave alone, and do it now.

###

While she pretended not to notice, she studied many of the random flashes aimed at her and Tommy. Being photographed with a legend would definitely help her career. Why he attended confused her. She assumed this was out of his norm. While his reputation of being extremely demanding and cold didn't seem to fit, she had watched him in action earlier in the staff meeting when he scolded her in front of the others.

As she worked her way to a side room, she watched the photographers following her. While they knew Tommy on sight, she felt sure no one knew who she was. As far as Joe was concerned, who knew? His family was rich and powerful in their own way, but he had always managed to stay out of the spotlight.

A tall woman marched toward her as she entered the reception area. "I saw you setting beside Tommy Conseco. I was really surprised to see him here today. Is he still here with you?"

"No. He had to leave. I think he totally enjoyed the show today. I know I did."

The woman still gave no indication as to who she was. Her larger than life hair style had been pushed to the limit. Balarie could only imagine how much spray it required to stay in place. The woman had oversized designer glasses which were so dark that they totally hid her eyes. *Is she an older model, an editor from a magazine or the competition?* She definitely reflected the flair of the fashion industry.

Balarie hated playing games and decided to make the first move. "My name's Balarie and I work with Mr.

Conseco by the way."

"Well, you answered my main question. For a moment I thought we might have finally discovered who his lover might be."

"I wouldn't know. I've only started with the company and from what I can tell he likes to keep his personal life separate and private." Balarie waited for the woman to introduce herself. She apparently knew much about Tommy Conseco, and things she might find useful.

"I'm Victoria James and I'm sure we'll get to know each other better. I'm the executive editor at Heartbeat magazines. We've used your agency on many occasions."

"I see. You should've said hello to him then. He just left."

"I'm sure we'll see each other soon. We both work the same party circuit. What are you doing at the agency?"

"I'm working as a booker and specializing in building our male model exposure."

"Good luck. That's a hard way to start. You have tough competition, but we need some guys often. Come by and see us soon."

"You can count on it. How does tomorrow sound?"

"Sounds fine. Come before lunch and

plan to join several of us checking out this new place. I have others on my team you should meet."

"Good. I'll see you tomorrow."

Joe walked over after she left. "She's one savvy woman but will play you all day long if you let her."

"What do you mean?"

"If she thinks you have something she can exploit, she will. If not, she'll feed you to the sharks at the other magazines. She appears nice to everyone, but she has hatchet men she uses to do her dirty work."

"How do you know this?

"I've been in the background for a long time, and I've learned to listen. She has been to my parents' parties for years, but doesn't even recognize me here now."

Balarie studied Joe and wondered about how his life had been in the shadows of his parents. With his parents so super flamboyant, how did he manage to be so different? But then again, she knew this often happened to kids of wealthy parents.

"I'll get us some wine. Hopefully they have something worthwhile here," Joe said as he walked off and left her open for others to approach her. She felt sure the brief time with Tommy made her a target. Perhaps that's why he came. If so, he acted like a sly fox.

Over the next hour she drifted from one person to another, making notes and contacts. Several people handed her cards, which was something she needed to have printed for herself soon. Everyone's focus shifted to her right. As she imagined, the designer made his way into the room. She knew he had spent some time with his inner circle before venturing to the reception area. While meeting him was one of her objectives, finding out more about his future plans remained imperative.

Balarie turned in his direction to study him working the crowd and accepting praises for his work. Minutes later he stepped in front of her. "I don't think we've met before, but I noticed you setting with Mr. Conseco. I sent word for him to join us in the back, but someone told me he had already left."

"He had to go, but he told me that he felt very much impressed with your work. I'm Balarie Danson, a new booker for his agency."

"Good. I'm glad you came, but we have almost no advertising budget."

"I understand. I'm a shoe fanatic and heard about this a few days ago and wanted to see your lines for myself. In case you don't know, Mr. Conseco is also crazy about shoes."

"Yes, I've heard. Perhaps one day I'll be able to meet him."

"I can arrange for you to meet him. In fact, he's having a party tomorrow night. I'll see to it you receive an invitation . . . if you're available."

"I'd love it."

"I know you're busy now, but it would also give us a chance to talk about your business more."

"Can you do me one more kind favor?"

"I might."

"On the invitation attach Conseco's shoe size. I might be able to bring him a surprise."

"I'm sure he would appreciate it. You created some very exciting designs I love."

"Thanks, which one did you like best?"

She didn't have to think long. "The one with a heel resembling a rail road spike sent images of power and drive to me. I think I connected with the overall design in it most."

"I was wondering how people would judge it. What size do you wear?

"I have big feet. I wear a nine and a half." She twisted her shoe to one side as he studied the shoes she wore. "It does help when you're this tall."

"Do you normally wear Jimmy's shoes?"

"I don't find myself loyal to any one brand. I guess I'm playing the market and always experimenting."

"Sounds like a good way to live life to me, but one day some guy will reel you in. You're much too pretty to avoid suitors forever." He reached over and held her hand while offering her a friendship style squeeze. "It was good to meet you tonight."

"And you too." She knew he needed to move along and say hello to his other guests. She had occupied a large chuck of his time.

With her mission accomplished, she hunted for Joe and soon found him talking to another guy. He waved at her to join them. "This is Barry, another one of the top photographers in the city."

She extended her hand toward him where he lifted it to his lips for a polite French style greeting. "Joseph was telling me about you. I gave him my card and hope we might be able to do some business together at some time."

"There's a strong possibility. I'm working on finding work for my models now."

"Stop by and show me what you have in your stables. I shoot for many advertising firms."

"I'm going to be making the rounds.

You'll see me soon."

She watched Joe give Barry a very intimate hug, sending the message that Barry must also be gay. With the afternoon disappearing, she needed to hurry back to the office to start setting up interviews with the models she would be pushing. Meeting them in person would make her job so much easier.

Chapter 5

Joe worked the phones as Balarie studied the database of photos from the computer on her desk. Selecting the best images to use in promoting them proved to be a challenging chore. While each generated their own personality and style, it was their versatility that added to their chances of being used. But nailing a specific look also locked out the competition when they needed such. Still, and most of all, the model must be the one who lodged in the buyer's mind until needed.

Studying one stud after another had its moments. While she tried to stay immune to their magnetic desires and not fantasize, she failed often. Seeing them in person would be harder. As one who loved the gym, she also loved the effort required to maintain such a rock solid body.

Joe walked in. "We have a problem. Brett Gould, a designer, is on the phone and upset. A model he used before arrived for a photo shoot. The model has bulked up since the last time they used him and he's upset. He's on line two."

She grabbed the phone and clicked on the line. "This is Balarie. I understand we have a problem."

"You're fucking right, we do. I should've been given new photos of this model since he has a totally different look now. Not that it's bad, mind you, but it's completely not right for my look."

"Mr. Gould, I do apologize. This is my second day here and the previous booker scheduled it before I started. I can send a back up there shortly."

"No, it's too expensive to sit around. Come see me and bring me some new photos of guys you have available which represent a solid college or young fresh professional image."

"I can be in your office in an hour."

"Okay, I'm waiting on you."

She decided to go with what she knew. She rushed through her top choices. Most of them were bulky. *What happen to a full line I can present?* She needed to talk to the girl in management about the models. She needed different guys to select from.

She yelled at Joe as she slipped her selections in a case. "I need to go. Stall my appointments for me. I don't think I'll be gone long since their office isn't far from here. And do me one

more favor, searched the data base for someone cute and normal, not bulky. Text me with any names you find."

As she rushed to the door, she added one more request. "Set up a meeting with the girl hiring these models. We need to talk about diversity."

Balarie hurried to cover the three blocks, but she knew the four inch heels could easily break if she ran. She controlled the pace as she thought of the models she had reviewed so far. This could be a problem. She now knew where she needed to spend some time.

A few block over she received a text. "I have two names and their files attached. Good luck."

Two names—that's all! She felt the hot, city air overtaking her. She didn't need to rush in all sweaty. She slowed, as she pondered her presentation. She needed to pitch it as the best she had and would follow up with others soon.

Minutes later, as she entered the design studio, she came face to face with a skinny guy with large, black rimmed glasses. Perhaps in his early thirties, but totally bald, he looked different from what his voice had projected.

"My name's Balarie Danson. I hurried

as fast as I could."

He lowered his glasses. "Damn, you must have run all of the way."

"Almost, I knew you were in a hurry."

"I'll have to say this is far different from the last booker we worked with. What do you have for me?"

"Since I know you might be behind schedule I selected the two you might want to consider. Shall we go to a conference room for you to look at these?"

"Absolutely." He motioned for her to follow him.

The first guy she showed him made him smile. "He'll do perfectly. If you can get in touch with him we might be able to save some time. The photographer is still next door working on another project."

"I'll do my best." She located the number and made the call.

A young sounding kid answered the phone. "Hello."

"This is Balarie calling from Conseco Modeling. I have a job for Brian."

"I'm Brian. You're kidding. What kind of job?"

"I never kid. The only condition is that you must to be able to come to work like right now."

"I can shower and shave and be ready in fifteen minutes if that's fast enough."

"Perfect, here . . . write down this address. I'll be waiting on you to arrive and I'll have an invoice for you to use. Hurry!" As Balarie repeated the address, she knew she had made his day.

Balarie glanced at the buyer. "I'll stick around until he arrives if you don't mind. I want to make sure we take care of you."

"I'm impressed. We have a new collection we're working on. We need to sit and talk about it. Bulky guys don't work for us."

"I understand. I'll see what other models we can find for you."

"Good."

Balarie smiled as she thought how this would be her first billing. The previous contract would be cancelled and a new one entered, giving her the commission on this sale.

After watching the new shoot come off without a problem, she left and returned to the office where Joe held it together for her. With several models waiting on her, she would make this quick and get them on their way.

As Balarie brushed pass them, she smiled. "Sorry I'm late, but we had a small emergency. Who's first?"

"Hi, I'm Christopher." The tall, dark-haired guy on the end stood. His short and neat hair cut gave her the impression he must have been in the army for too long. His muscular body reiterated what she already knew. The girl recruiting the male models had a thing for a certain kind of guy. Still, he looked like the kind of hunk most girls drooled over.

"Thanks for coming in on such short notice. I started yesterday and want to meet everyone so I can better recommend you and hopefully find you some work."

Balarie closed the door behind them as he walked over to a chair in front of her desk. He waited for her to reach her desk. Being raised in the south she appreciated the show of respect.

She opened his file as he leaned forward from his chair. "How long has it been since you updated the photos in your file?"

"I think it has some new stuff. I wish more. The work has fallen off recently, which is probably why the previous girl is no longer here."

"I'm learning a little about her, but she's not my concern, you are. What have you been hearing from clients you're working for?"

"I guess the usual. They're always looking for the next new guy to promote their stuff."

"Understood. Which clients do you like

working with the most?"

"If I could bulk up more, I would love cover work for health magazines or even a vitamin or equipment sponsorship would be great."

"The competition for those can be great and the pay is high, but limited. How about slimming down and doing more business shots?"

"It doesn't matter to me."

"Good we almost lost an account a few minutes ago due to one guy being too bulky for the shoot."

"Really?" The surprised look made him raise his hand to his chin.

"Yes, that's why I'm late." Balarie continued to study the photos in front of her. "I'll see what I can find you for now and we'll get back together in a couple of weeks. I'm going to be talking to a lot of buyers to see what their thoughts are."

"You're different."

Should she take his comment as a compliment or an insult? "In what way?"

"No one else has asked my opinion on things before."

"The feedback I obtain from you will help me enormously in finding you new jobs. Let's work as a team."

He offered her a large grin. "Thank you very much." She made a note of his manners. This would go a long way in helping his career. As he stood, she surveyed his shape once more. His rugged hard body sent waves of pent up desires flowing, but she had learned the trick to turning them off. She forced herself to think of him as a product.

As he walked out, the next guy walked in and settled in the chair facing her. "Hi, I'm Rick."

She smiled at another guy with muscles, but this one offered a different appeal with his long, blond hair flowing over his shoulders. He offered the bad boy image that many girls couldn't resist. "Wow! I wish I had your hair."

"It pays the bills, but it takes a lot of time to manage. I heard they hired someone new. I sure hope you have more contacts than the previous booker."

"Tell me about your latest work and what you would like to do." Balarie started getting a bad feeling about this previous booker and the bad will she may have created. She would love to ask Tommy more about it one day soon.

"I've one photographer who uses me the most. He's building stock files for e-book covers."

"Have you worked any book covers for romance novels?"

"No, but I would love to."

"I'll see what I can do for you." She grinned and analyzed his look. The thoughts of having sex with him floated across her mind, but it disappeared quickly as she adjusted her focus on the business in front of her that she needed to address. One night stands weren't for her, but she hadn't had a boyfriend in a while.

The meetings progressed, but remained short and to the point, which was exactly as she had planned. She needed to know how out of date the photos looked and how hard or easy the models would be to work with.

Joe stuck his head around the corner. "Don't forget you have a party to go to tonight?"

"I almost forgot. Oh crap, I was supposed to invite the designer from yesterday."

"Not to worry, I have already handled it. And I have a surprise for you."

"What?"

Joe handed her a box. "I can only imagine what would come in a shoe sized box from a designer."

"You're kidding me." She squealed but managed to hold it under acceptable OSHA limits. She remembered the last time she confronted Tommy as she ripped off the cover. Her eyes blinked in disbelief. These were the ones she commented on the day before. "Wow!"

Joe lifted one of the shoes from the box. "You can say that again. These are worth much over a thousand."

"Not really?"

"Really, where are you planning on wearing these?"

"I think tonight will be fantastic if I can find something to match from my pitifully small wardrobe."

"Well, he'll be at the party tonight, and I'm sure he would love to see his design making the rounds."

"You're coming tonight, aren't you?"

"I don't think so. I made other plans."

"Have fun." Balarie grinned, thinking about what he had planned.

Balarie knew Joe went to enough parties to get bored with them. However, his adventures would be much more fun, but not for her tonight. She needed to make an impression, meet people, and see what Tommy had planned for her.

Chapter 6

Balarie walked out of the elevator and into the party hosted inside Tommy Conseco's penthouse condo facing Central Park. While she knew he was wealthy, she was totally unprepared for what she experienced. The ceilings stretching over fifteen feet high allowed massive paintings, as well as countless art objects, to be displayed on many walls. Lights twinkled from several huge chandeliers hanging overhead.

A doorman stopped her as she wandered in. "Can I help you?"

"Hi, my name's Balarie Danson. I work for Mr. Conseco who invited me to a party here."

The expression changed on his face instantly. "It's good to meet you. I'm Peter and I handle Mr. Conseco's home for him. Please make yourself at home since he's planning a large turn out tonight. You'll see him inside."

"Thank you." She walked around as she studied the crowd and hoped to find someone she knew. From across the room, she studied several shifty eyes from people analyzing her. Yes, a drink would definitely be in order.

Her walk attracted the interest of one person—Ethan. The agency photographer she had met earlier walked over to her. "I thought you might be here tonight."

"How are you?" Balarie studied the artsy looking photographer she met earlier whose appearance had now been replaced by a more dashing, charismatic gentleman. "It's good to see you clean up nicely."

"It's all part of the job. We actually have much in common interest." He swirled a drink in front of him. "But first, allow me to find you something to drink."

She accepted his arm and walked to a bar area in the next room. The black bartender working behind an elaborate wooden bar smiled at her with teeth so contrastingly white she paused to study him. His tux looking outfit made him appear extremely professional. "What can I get for you tonight?"

"What kind of wine do you have?"

His grin increased as he pointed behind him. "Almost anything you want. Mr. Conseco keeps a fully stocked cellar behind here."

Who keeps a wine cellar in a penthouse?

She gasped as she watched him open a side door to a large room with racks of wine neatly stored inside. "Amazing! If you have a French Bordeaux you could recommend, I'd be very happy."

"I think I can handle that request." He located a bottle and quickly handed it to her. "What do you think?"

"I think it needs to be set free."

"I like the way you think."

As she accepted the glass, she turned to Ethan and touched her glass to his. "I think I can love working for Tommy."

"I see. You're already on a first name basis with him."

She froze for a second and wondered if she made a mistake in using his first name. "I just started to work for him and have only met him a few times. What does he want most people to call him?"

"Privately he prefers Tommy, but in public he likes Mr. Conseco. He has an image to maintain like everyone. I've known him for a very long time."

"And all of his deep, dark secrets."

"Secrets are a commodity friends know how to keep."

She glanced around the bar to study those around her. "I guess I need to mingle for a while. I think that's why he invited me to the party."

"Sometimes going after people is great. Making them come to you is extraordinary. Allow me." He pulled her by the hand to another room where many people had gathered. As he introduced her to selected people briefly along the way, she noted the brief teasing type intro he was offering.

"I'm going to leave you here, but I'll be close enough by to rescue you in a minute."

"Rescue me?"

"You'll see." He kissed her hand and walked off. Yes, he made her a sitting duck for everyone to venture over to. She lifted her glass and enjoyed a long swallow. She preferred to take the lead and not wait, but decided to follow his advice.

Two older women soon joined her. "How are you tonight? You must be Tommy's new girl we've been hearing about."

Balarie considered the question and assumed they meant the new member of the management team at the agency. "Yes, you can say I'm brand new."

"I'll have to say that I admired the great photo of you with your boyfriend in the paper today. I think you make a good looking couple."

"What photo?"

"The one taken of you talking together at a fashion show of some kind yesterday."

Now, she understood and remembered. "Sorry, but I think you have the wrong idea. I'm not his girlfriend. I work for him." She forced a giggle to lighten the situation.

One woman turned to the other. "I should've known better. He has always managed to hide his personal life before."

"It sounds like you know him well." Balarie attempted to analyze this woman, but failed.

"I think everyone has heard of him, but no one knows him well. I think he does that on purpose to frustrate us."

While talking to them, Balarie heard noise coming from the next room. As she shifted her attention to see what was going on, she managed to hear one last remark. "That must be him coming now." Other conversations around the room also ended.

Tommy entered the room with a girl on both arms and two more following him closely. They all looked like supermodels and Balarie could only guess that they worked for him. The two following him dropped to the side to talk to a small group of other girls who looked like models as well.

As Tommy approached various people, the girls on his arms allowed him room to talk. This looked so staged that it was funny, but she knew better than to laugh.

Ethan moved beside her from out of nowhere. "It's time for him to make his entry. He'll be over to see you in a minute. The more time he spends with you here, the more people will come to see you. This is what I mean about having people come to you. So, let's see how good you are in attracting his attention."

Okay, now she understood as she thought fast. "I understand you photograph people but have you ever photographed products, like shoes?"

"I have on occasion. Why?"

"Have you even noticed the shoes I'm wearing?"

Her questions made him look, which is exactly what she wanted. As he leaned over for a better view, she caught the side glance of Tommy studying the photographer. That's all she needed.

Ethan stood taller as he moved closer to her. "I know shoe fashion, but don't remember seeing this pair before. Where did you buy them?"

"I didn't. They were a gift."

"I see you're learning fast. Tommy does concede a weakness in shoes. I hope you get the chance one day to see his collection. It's one of a kind."

Balarie would love to see them. Getting

into the inner circle of the company would make her chances of survival much more likely. She harbored no illusions in how often the staff turned over at a modeling agency. She had to take off swimming or drown.

Tommy grinned as he walked over and shook Ethan's hand. "I see you two have met. I hope both of you can generate some good business soon. This market sucks right now." He faced Ethan. "Make sure you introduce her around for me."

"I think she'll be a hit here. She already saved our butt once today."

"Really." Tommy turned his attention back to Balarie. "That was quick."

Balarie leaned closer to whisper. "I received a call from Brett Gould, the clothes designer who wasn't too happy with one of the models sent to do a shooting today."

Tommy leaned closer as his voice lowered. "What?"

"The model had added some weight working out and presented the wrong look for his line. I found a replacement he liked."

"Good, so all's under control now."

"Yes, he's very happy." Balarie allowed the feeling of accomplishment to radiate in a smile.

Tommy glanced at her feet. "I noticed you're wearing a fascinating pair of shoes."

"Yes, a gift from yesterday. Aaron Chinell, the designer I met yesterday, appears to like me. I invited him to the party and cleared it with your assistant, but I haven't seen him yet."

"I'm sure he'll show and it's a good move on your part. I host these parties often and you can use them as a tool. I do." He glanced once more at the shoes. "Nice . . . very nice."

A quick wink and he moved on. Two steps away and Balarie watched the sideways glance back at her. He returned to whisper in her ear. "I have some shoes that I think you would like to see. Look for me later."

"Yes, sir."

He smiled at the use of *sir*. As his rugged, masculine persona penetrated her thoughts, she knew he was a master in timing by hesitating not too much or too little. He finally offered her a grin before continuing around the room.

The photographer nudged closer to her. "I think I may have underestimated you. I think Tommy has an interest in you."

"What kind of interest?"

"That remains to be seen. Being invited to see him later is a rarity—trust me." He glanced at her glass. "How was it?"

"It wasn't bad. I can get used to it."

He laughed. "I've tried it before. Do you mind if I share a glass with you, it would be a shame to allow such a bottle to go to waste, especially at that price?"

"Why? How expensive is this wine?"

"The last time I checked it was over one thousand."

One thousand, he had to be kidding! Her eyes focused on the glass. "I hope he's not going to be upset with me selecting it."

"Not at all, he can be extremely generous to his guests. The people in this room are what make money for him, and he knows that. He's clearly expecting big things from you. I can feel it."

Balarie followed Ethan back to the bar, knowing he had the secrets she needed to learn to make it in this company. She needed to limit it to the next glass, however, since she wanted to meet many people and remember their names tomorrow.

As they returned to an outer ball room, Balarie saw Aaron walking toward her. A flash of excitement shot through her body.

"I hoped you would come." Balarie wanted to hug Aaron's neck for the gift, but forced her body to maintain control.

"I see you're wearing them. How do

they feel?"

"Fantastic. Mr. Conseco noticed them also and commented on them."

Aaron beamed. "Wow! That's the kind of compliment I love to hear."

She turned to her side to introduce Ethan, as they sized each other up. Aaron's attention soon returned to her. "I also have a present I worked all day on for Conseco. Is he close by?"

"We saw him a few minutes ago, and I'm sure he'll want to see you." She turned to Ethan and handed him her glass. "Where do you think I can find him?"

Ethan pointed to his left. "I'm sure he'll be in the next room." He paused for a second. "It's getting late for me. Enjoy the party. I have to line up some shots for tomorrow morning."

She offered him a small hug. "I think I owe you for helping me tonight."

"I do like being owed," he chuckled as he left.

Balarie offered her arm to Aaron. "Let's go to find him."

She assumed Tommy would be very happy with such a gift. Many people stopped her as she hunted for him. Finally, on a small balcony she saw him leaning against a wall with a drink in his hand, and the two beauty queens close by. She could only imagine what he had in store for them later, but maybe not. He said he never screwed the models, or in his words anyone involved in the fashion industry. That remained to be seen.

Tommy looked in her direction as she approached him, and a smile quickly erupted as he recognized Aaron. "How are you tonight? I'm glad to see you made it."

"Thanks for inviting me. I've heard of your place forever."

"Thank you, and feel free to look around."

Aaron nervously glanced at Balarie. "After talking to Balarie, I decided to try designing something special for you. I hope you like it." He handed Tommy the shoe box.

Tommy handed his wine glass to one of the girls he had been escorting around and lifted the top. His eyes twinkled as he studied one of the shoes. "How did you know I love this style? I think someone has been doing their research."

The bright, brass, Cuban heel dominated Aaron's design as he spoke, "I added a special composite material to the bottom of the shoe, making it both durable and great for dancing. It shouldn't hurt a wooden floor, but still make a great sound when it's danced in."

"I like them. What's this material?"

"Again, it's a composite of many. For the comfort of the ankle, I used deer skin, and for the toe I used Italian leather. I positioned the ornaments in places which will not obscure your ability to dance. My thought is to capture a great male dancer's main objective, which is much like showing off a great dancing partner. This shoe will hold the attention of the judges without distracting from the dance itself."

"You must be a dancer yourself."

"I have on occasion, but studying dance has given me a unique opportunity to study feet and their movements."

Tommy lifted the shoe higher. "I think I understand now why you're so successful. I've heard you're thinking about expanding, and I think we should talk soon."

"Whenever you're ready please have Balarie contact me and I'll be very happy to meet with you."

Tommy turned to Balarie and glanced at her shoes. "I saw hers earlier. You have an intimate relationship with heels. It's good to have such a trademark." He passed the shoes on to one of the models by him who was also admiring them. "Thank you again. Please help yourself to a drink and please mingle with my friends."

Aaron turned to Balarie and his eyes offered the best *thank you* she had received in a while. "Which way is the bar?"

Balarie knew she had made a good friend as she pointed the way but considered other plans, since she needed to find the restroom. As she watched one of the beauties walking away from Tommy, she assumed this model needed to visit there also. If she modeled for the agency, it would also give Balarie a moment to talk to her.

Both girls stopped outside the restroom. The girl talked first. "I saw you talking to Conseco. You must be new. I'm Marian Fitch."

"Yes, I am. My name's Balarie Danson and I'm a new booker with the agency."

"That's good to know. I keep hoping to land some good paying jobs. I think Conseco likes you."

"What makes you think so?"

"He talks to you. He hasn't said a word to me all night. I'd give him head right now for only a few words of encouragement."

"Do you think personally servicing Conseco would make a difference?" Balarie felt sorry for this girl with her priorities all screwed up.

"Hey, I'm just talking. I know he has any woman he wants and at any time." The door opened and another woman walked out. "I'll not be long."

Instead of waiting, Balarie decided to walk around for a while. While stopping to talk to several people along the way, she explored his luxury condo which appeared to go on and on forever. She soon lost track of the time.

She passed through a large kitchen staffed by two people dashing around and working on snacks. They paid her no attention as she explored further. Delighted in finding another bathroom she entered and examined the massive room. She had no doubt this functioned as Tommy's personal bathroom from the masculine design of colors and textures. A painting of a fully naked woman hanging on the wall definitely confirmed it.

She wanted to snoop, but forced herself to avoid the temptation. The shower, large enough to hold an entire basketball team featured a beautiful Italian style marble encasing it. A large stack of magazines rested on a table by the toilet. She could imagine him working in here as she giggled thinking about it.

Time continued to slip away as she realized she needed to return to the party. She glanced at the several doors leading out of the room. She opened the one she thought she had entered. Wrong room! She walked into a dressing room which was perhaps twenty by twenty. How could she resist? One wall consisted of

shoes on top of shoes, perhaps into the hundreds. Yes he definitely loved shoes.

She heard a noise and panicked as she rushed back into the bathroom. She listened but heard nothing else, however, the noise sounded real.

She marched to another door and peeked outside. Was this the way she came? She walked several more steps as she soon examined an exercise room of some sorts. This stuff looked nice—much better than the gym she frequented. Intrigued, she approached an exercise bike sporting complicated electronic attachments.

A voice suddenly started her. "You're looking at one of the most advanced training bikes in the world."

Gasping, she turned to see Tommy standing behind her, wearing only a pair of gym shorts. "Sorry, my bad, I got lost."

"The doors back to my private quarters are supposed to remain locked. I'll have to check on what happened later, but since you're here, what do you think?"

"I'm stunned. This looks world class."

"I saw you studying the exercise bike." He walked over and placed a hand on it.

"It's a one of a kind designed for me. The same people who created exercise bikes for Lance Armstrong did this one. It measures every part of your exercise and gives you feedback."

"I'm sorry to intrude. I wish my gym looked like this." She edged toward the door she entered from."

"You don't have to leave. I could use the company tonight. I'm going to use the step machine for a while to burn some calories, but you're welcome to use the bike if you want."

"I would join you, but I didn't bring anything to wear."

"You can strip down to your underwear if you wish. I don't think I'm going to hit on you, and I've seen my share of naked bodies in my life. I think I'm fairly well immune by now and being a model before, I know you shouldn't be shy."

With his comment pretty much straight forward and honest, she relaxed. "We met like a day ago."

"This isn't a date or a love connection. I'm sorry, I thought you were more into exercising than I assumed."

"Oh, I'm deeply involved with working out and staying healthy."

"Good, then show me what you can do. The machine will give us the answer if you put it in test mode. Do you think you can handle a steady session of say one hour?"

"One hour has never been a problem for me."

"Good, you pick your level and we'll see what the machine says."

Balarie studied him again. He wore a pair of plain, black gym shorts which extended to his knees. His broad, bare shoulders were ripped with muscles, and of course, he had the signature six pack many body builders loved to show off. While still short of competition level, he had the makings of a true devotee.

"I still have no shoes." She preferred not to do a strip tease for him, but considered the invitation.

"It's safe enough to use your barefoot on, but it's up to you. I need to get busy, so if you'll excuse me."

With his face turned to one side while he adjusted the controls to the step machine, she struggled with her answer. She never considered herself shy before, but she never considered herself a slut either. She fettered with the button to her top. Where would this lead?

Tommy added a plug to his ear to listen to music. He had left the decision up to her and appeared to care less if she followed through or not. She watched his muscles expand and contract. A slight shimmering glow to his body indicated he had already started perspiring as he ramped up the speed.

She unbuttoned the buttons to her blouse. Soon, the light jacket slipped off her shoulders, followed by the blouse. She wore a nice bra with ruffles, one of her favorites. She planned to keep it on. She walked to a side chair to sit while she removed the shoes, these she would treat with kid gloves for a long time.

She glanced at Tommy again. He never changed his position as he kept the same pace going. She stood and unfastened her belt. She knew she moved slowly as she struggled with misgivings. As she snapped the latch and unzipped her pants, she knew there would be no turning back. Still, she told herself, this was to exercise and wouldn't lead to sex. Surely not!

When her pants hit the floor, she stepped out of them and reached over to retrieve them. She didn't need them to wrinkle while she worked out. She glanced at the tread machine directly in front of her. He would have a good view of her without any effort, but she would need to shift to see him.

Her panties barely covered anything, and like many girls who modeled, she was clean shaven. She stepped forward and centered the bike as she studied the controls. A minute later, she set the programmed test for one hour before adjusting her speed for a medium test. She wanted to impress him, but also wanted to make damn sure she lasted the hour.

Even without seeing his face, she felt him watching her, and perhaps secretly ravaging her almost naked body. Again, it could be wishful thinking. How was she really to know?

As her body warmed to the steady strain, she enjoyed the rush she always received when her body perspired and a sure sign she had started burning calories. She glanced at the controls. She had fifty minutes to go. A screen in front of her showed the first hill she had to climb as she felt the strain increase slightly.

Free to think while she peddled, she allowed her mind to wonder. Her dreams of making it big in the city almost never happened. She wanted to pack up so many times and leave. She had worked in Miami for a year earlier and always planned to return to the sunshine state if she needed to. She could make a living in South Beach if she needed to resort to it. Selling what she owned in New York would be easy.

She laughed slightly, as she didn't even

own a car any more. She had no need of one in the city. If she moved back to Miami, she would have to rent one to drive to Florida since there was no way she would fly. Driving would be okay. Would she ever conquer her fear of flying? She doubted it.

The first hill didn't feel bad at all. She rested, as she adjusted to level land again. She wanted to turn toward Tommy again to see if he was watching her. A quick glance would be fine. She stretched the limits of her vision in his direction. His face remained straight ahead and his eyes barely open. He must be deeply into the music.

She turned her head to obtain a better view. He continued to climb the stairs, a feat much more strenuous than her bike. Out of pure curiosity she studied his body again. His firm middle core reflected his diet and exercise program. Many guys his age showed some signs of a growing midsection. She knew he was approaching the magical age of forty. This fact had been played up often in the tabloids. The big question often posed concerned his personal life. Would he marry before turning forty? Was forty the age he quit being the sex symbol for the city? The magazines always wanted to place him with some mysterious woman. She had no doubt he fed this media mill to maintain his image as the topmost eligible bachelor in New York.

The perspiration was now dripping down his body like liquid gold and darkened his trunks. With his body creating a natural glow, a radiance of raw sexual energy, it made it hard for her to look away. Without hesitation and especially since he paid no attention to her, she focused on his gym shorts, and more specifically on his crotch. Did he wear boxers under his gym shorts? Since he was getting his eyes full, she thought she should receive the same privileges. She wondered how big he was.

She heard a beep and glanced at the screen, which indicated she had a much larger hill approaching. The elevation increased and she felt the stress rise which made it much harder to maintain her speed. Her heart rate shot higher.

She glanced back at Tommy. She thought she saw a smile curling out of the side of his mouth. Her concentrations on his lips lead to new fantasies. His mouth looked strong and rugged, and the kind of mouth which proved to be a dynamite kisser.

The hill kept rising as she pushed forward. She had to be at the top of it, or something was wrong with the program. As she started to waiver, the hill eased and leveled out. Only twenty minutes to go.

She turned to face Tommy again. He kept pumping along as if he were some kind of diesel running at peak performance. He sweated profusely now, and it was the only sign of the heavy excursion. Perhaps he was a super man like she had heard.

She heard several beeps and watched a monster hill approaching on the screen. *You have to be kidding me.* She

glanced at the remaining time of fifteen minutes. She could make it while Mr. Cool trotted along. A quick glance at her heart monitor made her worry, however, as she knew that one hundred and seventy topped what she could do. She had worked out in gyms for a long time. She wasn't imagining things—the rate of tension increased again.

With five minutes left she reached her limit. She needed to hit the stop button before she crashed. What kind of test was this?

As she reached for it, she heard him speak, "Don't. It will adjust, you'll see."

Her legs stumbled to keep pace as she gave it one last try. The end of the hill registered on the screen. She now had hope as she pushed on to see a downhill run to the finish line. Good. She needed to cool down.

The victory fireworks flashing on her screen excited her. The workout had been one hell of an hour. Tommy stopped and unplugged his earplugs. "Now we'll see how you did."

She continued to breathe hard. "I made it."

"This machine's programmed to make sure you make it, but it's also designed to see how much you pushed yourself. It automatically reads your output and adjusts to see what your upper level is."

"I'll admit that it was a hell of a work out."

"The person who invented this software must be an extraordinary manager. The key to getting the most out of any employee is knowing when they're coasting, and when to let them rest before they snap. Your effort is what the computer inside calculates."

She stepped closer to him. She still wore nothing more than her underwear which was now coated in sweat. She envisioned the sweat melting them together. She had to avoid this as the words from him, her boss, the day before replayed clearly. He allowed no sexual relationships in his company. But then why was he seducing her like this. *He was seducing her, wasn't he?*

She always waited for men to make the first move. If he truly wanted her, she doubted if she garnered the willpower or strength to stop him.

He pointed to a table with a computer on it. "Let's check out your results."

She walked in front of him. He could at least offer her a towel to cover with. Instead he placed a hand on her shoulder and helped guide her along. The power in his hand transferred to her muscles which were anticipating a massage, but none came.

He clicked on a button, and the printer sprang into action to provide the results. As he read them he spoke softly. "I think you did very well. We'll have to do this again."

"I would love to."

"There's a shower in the corner you're welcome to. I need to get some rest myself."

She turned to locate it before returning to face him. "Thanks, I do need to wash. I worked up more of a sweat than I thought I would."

He smiled with a small leaning in her direction. She moved in on it and kissed his lips—a small expression of a pinned up desire to be with a man.

He didn't kiss back.

She parted from him. "I'm sorry, it was

a sudden impulse."

He leaned closer with his eyes boring into her soul. "Never apologize for taking what you want and earned. Just be sure what you want is worth the price."

A remarkable warning, but fair—she had no clue what she might be getting herself into. "I think I've paid my dues to advance where I am so far."

"Getting in the door is simply the beginning. And you know how competitive life can be. I have high expectations on what you can accomplish."

Her body appeared to have no effect on him. She realized the years of working around models had dulled his reactions most men would have. Yes he acted very different. But . . . a challenge is what motivated her. There would be many more days ahead of them.

###

Tommy dropped his shorts and walked into his shower. It never gets any easier. Woman excited him in general, but Balarie

pushed him to the limit again. His walls of defense weren't near as strong as they used to be, and he was getting older.

As he adjusted the water controls, the hot streams pounded his chest. He needed relief as he glanced down to buddy, his pride and joy, which stood at attention.

Times like this made it hurt as it expanded to its limits. Why did he subject himself to times like this? He shouldn't have allowed her in his gym.

But then again, to prove to himself that he could remain in control, he did ask her to strip. He knew, or at least guessed, that she had the perfect body that he craved. Her breasts stood perfect with no sag. The bra she wore wasn't needed for support. While it only slightly hid her nipples, her sweat soon allowed him, for all practical purposes, to know their exact size and shape.

His thoughts made him ache more. She would have joined him in his shower, but he sent her away. How could he be such a fucking idiot? But still, he didn't need another law suit. He still didn't know her intentions fully. She acted aggressive and smart, other characteristics he loved. He couldn't get her off his mind. The more she exercised and sweated, the more her hair also curled. He had wondered before if she added the curl, or if it was natural. This proved it was all natural.

He remembered her walking in front of him, twitching her ass for him. It looked tiny, and to be honest kind of flat, but he could live with one such minor detail, just not sell it if she wanted to model. All models offered certain assets and flaws.

He closed his eyes and imagined her in the shower. He would be penetrating her next to the wall. Yes, it would be a mind-blowing experience. He felt the relief. Damn, it felt so good!

But it is such a shame that I can't be with her in real life. Or can I? Should I?

Chapter 7

With thoughts of Tommy invading her sleep all night long, Balarie had finally decided a few hours ago that she might as well be at work. A cup of coffee would definitely help, as she staggered to the snack room down the hall from her office. Since she still had a couple of hours until the office officially opened, she felt like she had plenty of time to do more reviews of the models working for them.

A big guy startled her as she entered the room. She thought she would be working alone this early in the morning. Tommy turned to face her. He looked perfectly rested and as charismatic as she remembered from the night before. She wished she had his ability to snap back so quickly. "Oops, I didn't know you were in here."

He laughed, the first time she remembered him actually laughing out loud. "I'm usually the first one here every morning. I didn't realize you would be such an early bird."

"Since I couldn't sleep, I thought I would come on in."

"I see. I made fresh coffee and it looks like you could use some."

Did she look that bad? "Thanks, I could use some. I wanted to learn more about our models this morning that I'll be finding jobs for."

"We have many, but only a handful who really make you money. You'll learn soon where to spend your efforts."

"I understand and I'll be going over billings this morning also. I want to make contacts with our top buyers as soon as possible. I plan on meeting with Samantha later this morning. She called me yesterday."

"Being one of our top clients, make sure she receives whatever she wants."

"We'll be discussing her future plans today, I'm sure. I do have one question however."

"Which is?"

"In reviewing the male models I see where most of them appear to be very bulky and not the . . . what I call the *all American look*."

"We've been concentrating on the fitness market. The magazines want guys to push health clubs and vitamins, not to mention work out equipment."

"I understand, but we're lacking in the part needed by a lot of fashion photographers and designers."

"Slicks can be a lucrative market but we don't have much success with them."

"I see. Perhaps I can change our success rate."

"Or go hungry. Plan your time well." He glanced at a clock above him. "Talking about time, I have to get busy myself."

"Thanks for the coffee." She studied his face. He was so clean shaven. He must spend lots of time on his skin. For a guy with a rugged strong muscular face it was unusual to find one so smooth and well textured as his.

"You're welcome." As he stepped closer to her for a second, she inhaled his scent, the same invigorating one she remembered from last night, and the one which kept her awake all night.

She focused her eyes to see him staring directly at her. "Are you going to be alright?"

Embarrassed, she stepped back. "Yes. I had something on my mind."

"I see. You need to schedule an exercise program for in the mornings. I think it will help." He turned and walked away.

Hey, while she normally worked out in the morning, she couldn't be in both places at the same time. She watched him walk. He had one of those big powerful butts she loved to watch, which contrasted so much to hers. No amount of exercising could ever help her rear and she never planned on sitting on silicone. Hell no, not her.

###

Tommy had come to work early since he first started the company. Very seldom did anyone match his early morning routine. The time alone gave him time to reflect on his growing empire, but also made for a lonely life. He had made the necessary background checks on Balarie when he hired her, but now he wanted to know more.

Inside his office he retrieved her records in the database and found very little. He went to Google and added her name to the search box. Since she modeled some, she would have a presence on the net. He ran down the list and studied several until he found a gallery of photos he clicked on. The photos looked professional, but he saw no major companies who had used her. Midlist models never made enough to make it for long.

One photo caught his interest. The half nude photo highlighted her breasts in a wet and succulently transparent top. Yes, she looked good, and the photographer captured a special moment. Not many photos mesmerized him, but this one reflected a special quality. He looked for the name of the photographer and found it at the bottom of the page. He would have to contact this guy. He was good and he might have more photos of Balarie.

With all he had on his mind to do, Tommy wondered why Balarie kept dominating it. "Enough of this," he whispered as he hesitantly closed the page after concentrating one last second on her smile and breasts.

Tommy glanced at his calendar and tapped his finger on an appointment to a body building competition. He had planned to attend, but now realized that he needed to make sure Balarie appeared with him. He wanted her to see the opportunities in this growing market.

Chapter 8

At her desk Balarie poured over the records all day. She wanted to know who had used their models and which ones. She also wanted to be on top of what they needed later. The breakdowns helped, but she wanted the word directly from the source.

She walked out to see how Joe was doing on his task. She had him building profiles on every potential buyer. Wherever they went, she wanted to know about it. She had to infuse her life inside theirs.

"So how is it going?" She watched him studying the computer in front of him.

"Wow, we're going to be busy. The one thing I love about the city is the parties. I'm working on invitations to the ones which matter most, however it's Wednesday night. We're still going to Stars tonight later, aren't we?"

Balarie smiled and glanced around to make sure no one heard his question. She leaned closer to whisper. "Not so loud."

"Alright if you want to keep it quiet, but

everyone has to have an outlet." Joe pushed his lips together to indicate he would not tell others."

"I don't know how I let you talk me into going to a male strip club."

"Because you love it as much as I do. Be honest."

"I love the excitement in the bar, but I think you're the one who has dreams about the men on stage."

"Well . . . are we going or not?"

"It depends on how tonight goes. I received an invitation to go to a hockey game from Samantha. I need to stop by for at least a while. She has a private box in the arena and wants me to meet some of her friends."

"Sounds brutal to me. Call me on my cell later. I still might go on my own if I have to." Joe lifted a package for her. "This came a few minutes ago for you. They want to make sure your passport is up to date."

"Why?"

"Well, this company does operate offices in Europe for beginners. I'm sure they'll have you jetting around soon."

Balarie's stomach tightened and her head spin fast. Working Europe would mean flying. There was no damn way she would ride on a plane. She accepted the package and edged toward her desk. She hoped to delay this for a long time. What would they say when she told them she couldn't go?"

Joe walked in behind her and shut the door behind him. "You look bad."

"Have a seat and let me tell you something no one is to find out." She tossed the package to one side. "I can't fly. I'm terrified of flying."

"Humm, this is going to be exciting."

"I hope to concentrate on New York and nothing else. If it means no promotions later, so be it."

"I'll try to find out what options you have quietly for you. However, you know the models here work internationally."

"Yes, but that doesn't mean I need to travel to Europe with them. I hope to get some help one day, but not any sooner than I have to."

"Good for you. Why are you scared of flying?"

Balarie hesitated. "I've thought about this for a long time and I know what started it. However, the fear has grown. I was a young girl when we went to a fair to enjoy some rides when I lived back in Georgia. One of the cables snapped on a ride, causing several kids to be hospitalized. I've never trusted mechanical things since. You don't know how hard it is for me to even ride an elevator."

"In New York?"

"I know, I know. I've worked through it, but not the flying."

"If you conquered part of the problem I think you'll do the rest in time."

Balarie looked at the package. "I think I have little choice." She hid her face in her hands. "With so much going on, I need to stall."

"Don't worry. Because you recently started with the agency, I would think you would have your hands full here for a long time."

"I hope you're right."

###

Tommy asked Olivia, his assistant one more question as she prepared to leave. "Did you send the package to Balarie on the travel requirements?"

"Yes, I gave it to her assistant a few hours ago." She gathered the files in her arm and prepared to leave. "It's a little early to take her on trips, isn't it?"

"Oh yes, but I want to be prepared in case we face an emergency situation like the one she handled the other day." In fact, he had many upcoming possibilities cross his mind, and getting to know her better would be good. She acted different than most of the girls from his past.

"Don't forget you have a hockey game shortly."

"I remember, but thanks for reminding me. I'm not planning on staying long since I booked an appointment with my physical trainer later tonight." He felt good about hiring BreAnna. She pushed him and didn't care who the fuck he was. However, she also let it be known she doesn't mind using enhancements. With his mind focused on getting buffy, it became harder and harder to turn her down, in spite of the fact he knew they would add to his problems.

"Have a good time and I'll see you in the morning."

Tommy closed his eyes again for a moment and daydreamed about Balarie. His manhood grew at the thoughts of her. It had been too long. He knew he needed a woman, and not just any woman.

Chapter 9

Balarie eased along the upper ring looking for her section. Thoughts of attending a hockey match before flashed through her mind. It never made sense to her why some guys thought it was a special treat to take a date to a hockey game.

She barely had enough time to change before she rushed to the game, but she had wanted to look sporty, yet professional at the same time. She really needed to expand her wardrobe.

Walking inside, Balarie quickly found Samantha. "Hello, I hurried as fast as I could to get here." Balarie offered her a hug and glanced around.

"Don't worry. You arrived at the perfect time. I arranged for you to meet many people tonight, but first we need to find you something to drink. What do you want?"

Using her training in sales she made direct contact with her eyes. "I'll have whatever you're having."

"You're a brave girl." She turned to a

waiter walking behind her. "We need another Jack on the rocks."

Balarie swallowed. *No shit!* She would be drunk in no time drinking straight whiskey. Most of the guests looked older and dressed more formal than what she had expected. Apparently, this was a cocktail party crowd instead of true hockey fans who came looking for a fight on the ice. She was learning fast.

The waiter extended the drink to her. "Here you go."

Here you go is right, she thought, as she lifted the glass toward Samantha. "It's fascinating to see you're into hockey. Do you know any of the players?"

"I've met several of them. I actually own a part of this team, a gift from my ex-husband. It drives him crazy. Divorce can be hell can't it. He should have been more careful where he dropped his pants, and I'm sure he'll be next time."

"I think I get the picture." This explains why Samantha hosted the party and why she expressed so little interest in watching it. It was one of those to be seen moments. Yes . . . she should've dressed differently. Balarie lifted the glass and tasted the first dose of liquid fire, which burned her throat on the way down.

How she finished the first glass

surprised her, but not near as much as the sudden appearance of another in her hand.

Samantha, in her flamboyant way, introduced her to many people in the magazine world. All of them wanted to know more about her, and who she represented in the agency they needed to know about. She forced herself to remember names, but trusted Joe would gather them for her. She would like to send notes to them and stay in touch.

When nature called, Balarie excused herself to look for the ladies room. She found the only one inside the box locked with someone else occupying it. She needed to go—now. She looked for the door leading outside and hoped to find one there. A few steps later she bumped into a tall man rushing along the hallway.

"Balarie, what are you doing here?" Tommy smiled while two tall blondes stood behind him.

"Samantha invited me to a party here." She pointed to the door she came from.

"I see. I'm in another one a few doors down. It's good to see you going after business so fast. I'm impressed." He waited for the girls to flank him. "I'm late, but why don't you stop by later before you go. I'm in the box over there."

"I might, but I don't know how late I'll

be staying. I came dressed, thinking I would be with a lot of hockey fans, instead of a cocktail party."

She watched Marian snicker slightly.

"I think you'll like this crowd a bit more than the one you came from, but you have clients in there with Samantha you should work with." Tommy straightened his lapel.

"Thanks. I do have lots of work to do. I'll see you in a little bit. Do you think I'm dressed appropriately for your friends?" She watched him look her over in detail. Was he enjoying himself, or just teasing her?

"This is a hockey game. You'll do fine." He extended an arm for both ladies and marched on toward the room. She wondered about his rules of not having sexual relationships with anyone in the modeling world. If he truly lived by his rule he had a constitution of iron. Now where was the damn bathroom?

###

Tommy opened the back door to the box and went inside as he attempted to flush the images of Balarie from his mind. Marian and Linda snuggled closer to him, exactly as they were paid to do. He knew he could have many girls wanting to be with him, but such would add too many complications. These professionals knew the score. Any modeling job they could land would be payment enough. Why did he think he needed them? He realized old habits were hard to break.

Several guys immediately joined him. "Hello, Tommy. I'm glad you could make it." The guys totally ignored the girls behind Tommy. Much like him, beauty only did so much, as they were more interested in brains.

Tommy studied the men around him, most of them older with the average in the upper fifties and sixties, the age of most successful businessmen in the city. But their physical shape, the large bellies and faces needing attention attracted his interest. Would he look like them one day?

One guy pulled him to the side. "I saw your photo in the paper yesterday with a new girl. What's the story?"

"What photo?"

"The one of you at a fashion show of some kind."

Now he understood. "I dropped by a shoe show the other day to see a designer recommended to me. By the way, he designed me some new shoes to dance in. I'll be having a dance soon and you should come."

"I can't dance, but you're side stepping the question. Who is she?"

"The girl in the photo is a new booker we hired. Her name's Balarie and she might stop by in a minute."

"Oh, I see." The guy gave a side smile as if he was in on something.

"Man, you have a dirty mind, but you know me better than that."

"Yes . . . I guess so. You don't know how lucky you are being single. These nights out are my only days to have any fun."

"I'll have to tell Janice what you said the next time I see her."

"Is that a promise?"

Tommy shook his head. "How long have you two been married now?"

"About thirty three years."

"And?"

"And yes she has put up with me this long. Still you always have great looking girls around you all of the time."

"Yes, but this is what I do."

"So you still want me to believe you never touch them."

"Never have and never will. That's a promise I made to myself the day I opened shop."

"I've never known you to lie before. It still has to be as hard as hell." He shook his head and uttered a low laugh.

"Yes. I'll admit it's not always easy."

He glanced at the game under progress. "Who's winning?"

\#\#\#

With the crowd around her quickly getting drunk, Balarie thought she needed to leave. She searched for the door and suddenly realized she had way too much to drink. As she studied Samantha, who'd indulged much more than she had, she realized that Samantha would probably never know she had left.

After finding the right door, Balarie remembered that Tommy had wanted her to stop by for a minute. Should she? She had consumed a lot of whiskey. It would have to be quick. Since she assumed they might be drinking heavy also, she really hoped Tommy had already left. She slapped her face several times to clear her mind before she walked in.

Many guys in the box turned to her. All of them held a drink in their hand. Where was Tommy? She stepped inside a few more steps and saw the two girls he came with. Balarie knew the less she spoke; the easier it would be to hide the fact that she was drunk. She planned to make a quick hello and an even faster goodbye.

As expected, Tommy stood near the girls. He turned to Balarie as she walked over. "There you are. I was hoping you would make it."

"I promised I would try to stop by before I left." She steadied herself, and now wished she hadn't joined him.

"How did it go with Samantha tonight?"

"It went well. They're still having a good time, but it's more drinking than I can handle."

She felt him move close to her. "I can see you tried to keep up with them."

"I usually drink wine, but never whiskey. I didn't realize how potent that stuff is."

"I think I understand. I forgot to tell you Samantha can drink like a Russian tycoon, and you'll never know she drank a drop. If you drank with her, you're one brave woman."

"I think we bonded some tonight, but for now, I think I do need to get back to my place."

She felt him moving closer, supporting her. "I need to leave also. Please allow me to help cover for you. We'll all leave together."

"I hope you're not mad at me."

"No. Not at all. Just follow my lead."

"Okay. I need to get downstairs and catch a cab."

"I have a car downstairs, and I'll take you home after I escort the two models with me home."

After forcing one step in front of another, Balarie managed to exit the room. From there, they moved her to an elevator. She remembered her training. This wasn't a time to relive her fear of mechanical things which can break. Balarie closed her eyes as the elevator lowered to the ground floor.

Balarie barely remembered dropping the girls off. She felt him shaking her. "I need to know your address."

She gave it as she realized she really screwed up on her new job. Would he fire her? It was too much to deal with. She would worry about it tomorrow.

Balarie felt the car come to a stop as Tommy instructed the driver. "Wait here. This might take me a while."

She struggled to make it out of the car. So embarrassing. She tried to count the number of drinks she downed. Was it five or six?

"What's your door code?"

"1771."

After walking out of the elevator, he walked beside her toward her door. "I also need your key."

Balarie handed him her purse. "It's on the top." She watched him open the door and reach for her again. She managed to flip a switch on the wall as they entered. "This is so embarrassing. I promise it will not happen again."

"I need to help you get to bed. Which way?"

"I think I can manage now."

Instead, Tommy lifted her and carried her. "I'm sure you'll feel much better tomorrow." He pulled back the covers and lowered her to the bed. She felt warm gentle hands undressing her. She started to object, but why should she? He had already seen her practically naked once.

The warm covers pulled over her settled her nerves. He acted much more like a gentleman than she could imagine. She needed to sleep. The last thing she remembered was a warm gentle kiss on her forehead.

Chapter 10

Balarie's head hurt worse than her stomach, which made it hard to decide if she should try another cup of coffee. The large red bull helped some as she needed to make it through the day. How was Tommy going to react to her this morning? She prepared the coffee pot in the snack room to brew as she heard footsteps behind her. With such a loud tap reporting each step, it had to be Tommy.

She turned to him, but kept her face lowered. He reached under her chin and lifted it. "You had one hell of a night."

"I hope I didn't embarrass you or the company. I've never been . . . like that before." She felt her stomach churn.

"I think we contained everything, so don't worry about it. You worked with one of our largest buyer last night. Since I should have warned you about her, I'll take some of the blame for you this time. Also, since I'm sure she had a lot to drink, I doubt she'll say a word."

"Thank you. I promise nothing but wine

in the future."

"I'm really surprised to see you here this early." He reached for the pot and poured a cup for himself and one for her.

"I know how it works. I need to post some sales on the board quickly. I want this job, and I'll do what it takes to earn my spot on the team."

"Good for you." He stopped as he reached the door. "The next staff meeting will be on Monday. This isn't too far away."

Balarie knew she had limited time. She had today and Friday to line something up she could talk about. Headache or not, she needed to work the phone today. "I'll be ready. I hope I can convince everyone we need to find more preppy guys instead of the bulky ones we have in abundance."

His eyes twinkled as he stepped back inside. "I hope so, I like having a coffee drinking buddy in the mornings. If you can find the jobs, we can find the models. I want you to see something also. Late this afternoon I want you to go with me to see a body building competition, and maybe you'll understand."

While she thought about turning him down and spending the time finding buyers who wanted models now, she knew better. "Okay, what time?"

"We can leave at three. It will not take long, maybe about an hour, for me to show you what I'm talking about."

"I'll be ready." She watched him leave, but study her as he did. Damn, she wished she could read his mind. He couldn't be mentally undressing her. He did that the night before. He could have had sex with her, and she would have been helpless to stop him.

She walked on to her office as she heard her cell phone ring. She glanced at the caller ID and saw Samantha's name. *Now what?* "Hello."

"How are you this morning?"

"I'm pouring down the coffee at the office. How about you?"

"You're already at the office?"

"Yes. I have several items I need to handle early."

"Wow! I downed too many drinks last night and had to be hauled home by some of the guys. I hope I didn't make a fool out of myself. I usually don't have anyone who can out drink me. I'm going to have to keep an eye on you."

Balarie laughed. "I usually don't drink whiskey, but I enjoy wine."

"Maybe my choice of a drink is my problem. Wine—huh. Anyway, the reason I called this morning is to ask your opinion on some ideas I'm working on. Can you stop by around lunch? We can talk while we eat and without everyone bugging the hell out of me so much."

"Sure, I can do lunch."

"I've some photos of some of your guys, but I want to see a better selection. Please see what you can do for me."

"Will do. I'll be over around twelve." She disconnected and squealed. Wow! She needed to quit doing that, as she wondered if he heard her again. While it was an established client, it would still count as a sale if she could book one of the models.

She poured though the company database looking for any possibilities. She needed more. Like it or not, she needed to go to the model manager who handled the men. She already made it clear from the meeting she didn't like her, but she had no choice other than to try.

Joe broke her concentration as he walked in. "I never heard from you last night."

"I'm sorry. I got plastered and needed to be hauled home last night."

"Do tell. By whom?"

"Mr. Conseco himself."

"Wow! How did that go?"

"I thought my screw up had ended my time here, but it's going to be fine. The person who got me drunk was one of our largest buyers, Samantha."

"You do look a little out of it. What can I do?"

"I'm having lunch with Samantha today. I really like to know more about what they have coming up and what they're buying. If you can do more research I would be happy."

"You got it."

"What are you going to be doing this morning?"

"Trying to find us some models that are not like Mr. Hercules." She pointed to the stacks of models they represented.

"Hey, these guys look good to me." He fumbled though the stack.

"If I understand Samantha correctly, she wants nice guys who are normal, run of the mill, but still good-looking guys. You know, the average guy who buys clothes, but isn't built like some overstuffed gym toy. Most customers generally want to know what the clothes will look like on them instead."

"I guess you're right."

"I need to see BreAnna Thompson, one of the male model managers, and see what kind of help I can get." Balarie stood and felt the pain of a persistent, dizzy headache, one which made her think that she should wait a while; but no, she needed to do this as soon as she could.

Balarie walked along the hallway looking for BreAnna's office. She remembered seeing the name on the door earlier. As Balarie imagined, BreAnna had a large office with a view, but she had worked with the agency for a while and had established herself. The door was cracked open. Perhaps she should have called first, but no, they were on the same team and she should have the right to check with BreAnna on something like this.

Balarie peeked in the office and saw her at her desk. BreAnna immediately looked up. "Can I help you?"

"Yes. I wanted to stop by for a second and see if you can help me."

"Sure. What is it you need?" BreAnna lowered her reading glasses and shook her long, dark black hair. Her high cheek bones revealed her own modeling past. While Balarie remembered her gleaming white teeth when she smiled, she offered none to her this morning, but only a business curiosity frown.

"I've been, of course, analyzing all of the models we have under contract and noticed one item. They all appear to be . . . so muscular, and none of them are what I would call regular trim fit models."

"The trim fit types do runways which we don't have much work for lately. If you can find work for them I can find some for you. Conseco is the one pushing the guys to add some muscle."

"I gather that from him. He's taking me to a body building competition today."

"Conseco is taking you?"

"Okay. He more or less gave me no option. He wants me to go with him."

"That's a first. He must really be taking an interest in you."

Balarie knew better than telling everything. BreAnna would flip if she told about working out half naked with him, or Tommy talking her home last night and stripping her before putting her to bed. "We've had a brief discussion on the male models, and he wants to convince me there's a market for them."

"You do have guts. I don't know anyone brave enough to challenge what he thinks." BreAnna tapped her bright red polished nails on the desk. "The fastest way to add models is to go to the modeling school and do some snooping. It's a long shot. I don't have much time to train someone."

"Thanks. I might look into it. I did visit the school for a few minutes the other day."

"Good! If you see someone good down in the school, I'll fast track them for you."

For the first time BreAnna smiled and allowed her brilliant teeth to radiate her smile.

"Thanks." Balarie turned and left relieved that it went so smoothly. However, she knew she may have started a rumor with Tommy, which was something else for her to worry about.

After glancing at her watch, she knew she only had a few minutes to pop downstairs, but she couldn't be detained for long. The slight exercise on the stairway helped some, but it could also be that the coffee was kicking in.

Balarie opened the door to the school and walked to the business office where she saw the girl from earlier smile broadly. "Hello, Balarie. How are you today?"

"I'm fine, but I need you to do me a favor."

"Sure. Name it."

"I have a need for male models who offer the all-round preppy look and not so bulky, if you know what I mean. I need them slim and healthy looking, and not like a body builder."

"Such shouldn't be hard to find. It's remarkable that you ask for them because most of the ones applying never get accepted."

Balarie realized much more was going

on than she had thought at first. "Do you keep photos of the guys who finish school here?"

"Sure. But the photographer on the floor above has newer ones he can share with you."

Great! This would mean another stop for her. "I'll see him in a second, but send anyone you can think of to Joe, my assistant, and he'll get them to me." She smiled in appreciation before glancing at her watch. Time was flying this morning.

Climbing the stairs burned more energy. With the night before physically draining her, this would have to be a fast stop. She rushed into a shooting where people scrambled everywhere. Bad timing. She saw Ethan, who barely acknowledged her, studying a model in front of him that was being prepared for a shoot.

Balarie had turned to leave before she heard him call her name. "Balarie, wait up."

Good. She would have a minute to ask him a quick favor. "I thought you might like to watch some of the models in action today."

"I wish I had time." She offered a brief smile. "The reason I stopped by is because I need your help. I talked to the modeling school where they told me you have many photos of the students and I need a certain look."

"Yes. I maintain a ton of photos. What are you looking for?"

"I'll have a better idea soon since I'm having lunch with Samantha in a few hours . . . but in a nutshell, I need guys who are slim and fit who will pass for the all American guy and not big Arnold, if you know what I mean."

"I'll see what I can do for you. It will be after five." He maintained his stare on her face as if analyzing her. "If you want, I can take some photos of you also. You'll need some to promote yourself here."

She felt flattered. "I still have my folio, but it could use some updating. We'll see what kind of time we have." She really needed the photos like now before lunch, but she would stall, knowing she would have access to them later.

"I need to get back to the camera." He flashed one last smile. She knew photographers had to keep a good reputation and be fun to work with since they needed to set the models at ease to produce their best work.

She hoped Joe would have some research for her when she climbed the last set of stairs. Thankfully, he handed it to her as she rushed in. "I think you'll find some of this intriguing. The most important stuff is on the top. I know you won't have much time, but try to read it on the sub. Call me if you have any questions. I'm taking a long lunch myself today."

"Really, where are you going?"

"Shopping with a friend."

She laughed at his references to *friend*. "Okay, but I need you some more before I leave with Tommy this afternoon."

"Not a problem. Enjoy your lunch."

###

Being ushered directly into Samantha's office added a degree of confidence that Balarie needed. Samantha looked tired while she remained in her seat as Balarie approached her. "I wish I was younger like you. These late night parties are killing my ass."

"Yes, but it was kind of fun, wasn't it?"

Samantha raised her head and grinned. "Yeah, it did feel good." She pointed to the oversized leather chair in front of her.

"We've not done this in a while, and I think it's time we attempted it again. It would be easy if the styles didn't change so much, but they do. I guess being on top of the fashion swings is what keeps us in business. Women always study magazines to see what's in vogue. Guys get their info a totally different way. I want to run a new series, however, on how to dress your guy for success."

"Sounds like a fun project." Fun—shit—it sounded huge!

"To pull this off I need guys who look all American, but still capture most girls' version of a dream boyfriend. This will be not so much how guys want to dress, but how girls want their guys to dress."

"We would love to be a part of this project."

"I don't need to spread this around yet. However, I would love for you to handle supplying all of the models for it."

"We would consider this a huge honor." She must be dreaming to have walked in on something like this. Something was going on she couldn't understand. Why her? But still, she loved it.

"I have people working on the looks and the clothes. I'm thinking of taking a different age each month for several months. This will spread out the work load." Samantha settled back in her chair. "I'm not sure Tommy told you or not, but I recommended you for the job you have now. You have more drive than anyone I've met in a long time, and you sure the hell drank me under the table last night."

"Tommy, umm Mr. Conseco has been nice to me since I started there. Maybe I know why now."

"Don't get me wrong. Tommy and I go way back, and I've seen him break many hearts over the years. I think this industry has made him somewhat callous, if you will. Trust me, when a man locks out all possibilities of love long enough, it's impossible to reignite it. Sadly, it happened to my ex-husband while we were married. I'll accept some of the blame. I'm not stupid."

"I think Tommy is like a really nice man. He has always acted professional around me. I doubt if we'll ever have a problem with any kind of an affair."

Samantha leaned forward and whispered, "Do you have any idea how many people have called him Tommy?"

Balarie froze with what she knew represented a blank staring expression.

"His mother, me, and now you."

"No way."

"Way." Samantha twisted in her seat. I don't get to play matchmaker often, so let me have my day."

The wheels began to turn. Was her dream of playing matchmaker what this was all about? "I think . . . Mr. Conseco has his mind on his career and nothing more. I also want to succeed."

"Don't let me upset you. I've done my

part and I'll let Mother Nature play her part now. Are you ready to go eat? I need a Bloody Mary or something to kill this damn headache."

Chapter 11

Tommy walked to the window overlooking the city below his office. Some things never change. He'd watched many great models come and go, carrying their reputations and visions of grandeur with them. Most failed at some point. Age has a way of screwing the best of careers. His muscles hurt from the exercise program he had pushed his body into. His clothes didn't fit like they used to.

Thoughts of the body building competition created good and bad images. He had enjoyed his status as one of the city's most eligible bachelors for a long time. It wasn't all it was cracked up to be.

His assistant knocked on his door and ended his analysis of life in general. "It's time for you to go. Shall I call Balarie for you?"

"No, I'm sure she's waiting on me. I'll stop by and head out with her in a minute." Tommy glanced at his wall of fame, wondering what he would do with another award. He had conquered almost every goal he had ever set for himself. "Please have my car sent around for us."

"Yes, sir. Have a good time." She appeared to know this was work, but how he also had a passion for bodybuilding lately.

He hoped he could convince Balarie how big the industry was growing. Funny, he never remembered the urge to prove anything to an employee in a long time.

Tommy strolled along the hallway as he watched several people eyeing him. Word must have gotten out that he planned to take Balarie. He heard much more than most gave him credit for. His cold stares allowed him to hide his emotions. It also allowed him to extract loyalty. Not knowing what someone thinks can be a powerful weapon when needed.

Tommy watched Joe actively working some files. He needed to remember to ask Balarie more about him. As a temporary employee, he paid Joe almost nothing. With the money his dad made, it was a joke he worked at all. Why was he so loyal to Balarie?

"Hello, Mr. Conseco. Balarie's waiting on you." He cleared his desk of some of the scattered files, but left a few open.

Tommy leaned over to examine some of them. "What is it she has you working on?"

"Balarie returned a few minutes ago. She has some good news to share with you."

"Good news is always a great thing. I gather her meeting with Samantha went well today?"

Before he could answer, Balarie walked through the doorway from her office. "Yes, it was extraordinary, but it may be a lot for me to chew. I'm going to need a lot of help."

Tommy felt a pride rising in him for her, but remained calm and collective. "I'm sure we can all pitch in."

"I'll tell you all about it as soon as the details are worked out. I hope I'm not late."

"No, we're right on time." He offered her an arm which was meant to be more of a play than reality. He was used to girls on them.

###

Balarie studied the gym which had been converted into a place to hold the competition. Her best guess assumed this had functioned as a basketball court at one time. Body builder types roamed everywhere, wearing cutaway clothes designed to highlight their muscles.

After seeing a row of tables lining the back wall, Tommy quickly moved to them. "This is part of what I want you to see.

This industry is large and expanding. You'll find many sponsors here from vitamins companies to health equipment, and not to mention the magazines which cater to it."

Balarie could see his point, but most of all, she could see the dedication of the guys who participated in the competition. On a far side, she also noticed women preparing for the competition. They were not as prevalent as the men, but were still there in significant numbers.

Perhaps she assumed wrong and needed to do more research. "Are any of the competitors under contract with us?"

"I'm sure we have some, but I don't know many of them personally. I let the managers handle them."

"How long will the competition last?"

"These are preliminary and practice rounds. The big tournament will happen in a couple of weeks."

Something else apparently caught his eye as he pulled her along with him. "I want to look at this also."

She saw a section with many exercise machines on demonstration. While he appeared to be examining them, she realized he slyly studied the models demonstrating them. They were possibly booked by a competitor.

Thirty minutes later Tommy still asked questions about how they worked and what kind of benefits they offered. She enjoyed the explanations as much as him, but also focused her mind on the big account she had landed—one he knew nothing about yet.

Appearing to be satisfied, Tommy turned his attention to another wall. "Come and see this. I think this is where you'll find some of the big endorsements."

Displays of vitamins and supplements lined the wall. Many bulky guys and muscled girls walked in front of them. She knew how much these could cost. She also understood how many people have become hooked on them, especially the steroid-laced ones which could also cause disastrous results.

At first, Balarie watched Tommy study the advertising, which she would expect. Then she watched him studying one bottle after another and reading the labels. She wondered what, if any, he had used.

A tall girl with muscular arms ventured over. "What can I help you with?"

"You have a large selection here." Balarie waved at the walls.

"This is nothing compared to what we carry back at the store." The woman glanced passed her and smiled. "You appear to work out some, but you need to add a little weight. Are you taking anything?"

"Usually a good diet, but I use vitamin supplements sometimes. I'm not too much into adding muscles. I simply want to stay health and active." Balarie motioned to Tommy. "I think he's into it much more than me."

The sales girl decided to move on to a better prospect. "I can tell you're hitting the gym some. The supplement you're holding is as close to a steroid as you can get legally."

Balarie spoke without thinking through what she was asking. "I heard many bad things about steroids. Aren't they dangerous to your health?"

"They've received a bad rap, and do create some side effects, but nothing which can't be covered with other supplements." She walked over to the wall and selected a small red bottle. "This is the best in replacing male potency and increasing lost testosterones."

Tommy glanced at the bottle. "Can I see that?"

Balarie held her breath and turned to look at other items on the wall, acting like she didn't know. She had heard the talk around the gym. Too much exercising and too much bulk, especially with the use of steroids made a guys penis shrink and made it almost impossible to manage an erection. Surely this wasn't Tommy's case, but it would explain a few things.

To Balarie's relief he handed it back to the girl. "I don't think I'll be needing this." Tommy offered a strong masculine smile to back it up.

A guy who knew Tommy marched over. "Mr. Conseco, I didn't know you would be here."

"Hi, I thought it would be good to check it out. I heard it would be packed."

"There is nothing much happening until the finals."

Tommy turned and introduced them.

The new guy looked confused. "What happen to the previous booker we had?"

Tommy stepped forward. "She's no longer with us. I hope Balarie can book you more appointments."

"I hope so also. I want to work. Please tell me what I need to do."

"I'm analyzing everyone's file now. What kind of work have you been doing?" Balarie asked.

"It has been spotty, but some for advertising firms lately. I want to work."

"How long would it take you to slim back down for some shoots?"

"Not long, what do you have in mind?" He locked his knees in place and leaned forward. She dominated his interest.

"Come by tomorrow morning and I'll explain it to you."

"You got it." He glanced to his left where another guy wearing the ruminants of a shirt joined him. "This is Marco. He's also with the modeling agency."

She examined Marco's body, another guy who definitely admired the sport. "How are you, I'm Balarie Danson, the new booker."

"Yes, I heard we hired someone new. Are you here to check us out?"

"In a way yes. Mr. Conseco wanted me to join him here today. It's an eye opener."

He glanced at Tommy and extended his hand. "I hoped you could make it today."

"I wish we could stay longer, but we wanted to make a fast stop by here." Tommy kept his back straight and head high.

"Please, while you're here let me escort you to a prime seat in front, I'll be performing in about five minutes."

"I think we can stick around for a minute or two." Balarie accepted his arm and watched the other guy walk around to the other, escorting her like some kind of queen or something. She knew it was all for show, but she enjoyed it.

As she turned to take her seat she studied Tommy's face of approval. She understood the message. He was grooming her in his image. However, was in his image what she really wanted?

Tommy joined her and pointed to the stage. "The amount of time these guys practice posing is incredible. The one thing I want you to concentrate on is how much this relates to modeling. It's different, but still an art form in its own."

Balarie remembered watching enough short presentations on TV to understand how it could be and this wasn't totally new to her since she occasionally ventured into male strip clubs with Joe, which was one secret she would always keep. She went for excitement, not so much for the guys.

She retrieved a small note pad she carried with her and made some notes. The week would be over soon. Tonight she would stay late at the office. She remembered the photographer's offer to take some photos. Personal modeling is one career her fear of flying had already killed. Still, she might book a job here and

there for some extra money. Nothing in her contract prevented her from such. She might need to fall back on it one day also.

Tommy touched her shoulder to draw

her attention to the stage. "He's up next."

The bodybuilder walked to the front of the stage and bowed to her and Tommy, as if honoring them for their presence. Soon a photographer walked to the front of the stage, obviously an amateur, but welcomed by some of the participants who wanted to have their photos taken.

As he hit one position after another she studied the choreography involved. She remembered studying ballet when younger and understood the same level of control he needed to learn. His muscles intrigued her, engrossing her with images she mixed with fantasies she had hid years ago. Making love to such a guy would redefine her images of sex all together, but still, she wanted so much more.

However, as she watched him perform, she found herself disappearing into a different world, one where pure raw sex overrode romantic feelings of endearment she had always treasured.

Without turning to her side, she knew Tommy was studying her and her reaction to the performance. Why was he doing this to her? Was he really testing her?

Balarie forced herself to make notes and control her breathing. She was a professional. She had seen hundreds of men before and she had allowed many see her almost naked in the studios while she was being photographed. Still, she had to admit she was still a woman, a woman with no man in her life for a long time.

With her eyes focused on her pad she jerked as a flash exploded in her face. Tommy nudged her. "Time to go, he just figured out who we are."

Balarie reached for her sunglasses and stood beside Tommy, who quickly ushered her ahead of him. "You need to get used to it." He reached for his cell phone. "Bring the car around, we need to leave asap."

This guy's attention attracted the others who wanted to get in on the action. Fortunately, several of the big guys came to their rescue and sheltered them as they walked out of the auditorium.

She followed his lead and kept her face frozen and looking straight ahead as a mixture of excitement and annoyance filled her mind.

Minutes later they rushed to the car outside. "I guess we can expect more photos of us in the media soon."

"It comes with the business. I'll have my assistant deal with it. So . . . what do you think about the body builders now?"

"I never said I wasn't impressed with them. I only wonder if we're missing a larger market in concentrating so deeply on them."

Tommy shifted in his seat. "I've one more event you need to attend and sorry about the late notice. Can you dance to the tango?"

"I learned it when I received some dance lessons earlier, but haven't practiced in a long time—why?"

"I have friends in town this weekend who live in Argentina who have invited me to come. I'll ask them to send you an invitation later tonight."

"An invitation to a dance is thoughtful of you. I really appreciate the interest you've taken in me."

"I see the potential in you, and I'm usually never wrong. You don't have much time to buy something, but they're a colorful group so do your best."

Her heart hit the floor. A dress—she had two days to buy a dress to dance tango in. She fought the urge to yell. "I'll do my best."

"I know you'll not disappoint me."

This time she wasn't sure. Should she turn him down or . . . oh shit—two days!

Chapter 12

After rushing down the stairs to the agency's photographic studio, Balarie wondered why oh why she did this to herself—she didn't need personal photos now. She had too many other things to do. Still, the excitement of new photos intrigued her. While she would love to model some more, she knew it would seldom happen, if ever, after she started working at the agency as a booker.

The studio felt quiet as she walked in and noticed that most of the lights had been turned off. "Hello." She moved cautiously forward.

She soon located Ethan who was on one side adjusting some equipment before he turned to her to speak. "Oh, there you are."

"Yes, I'm running a few minutes late. We went to a body building competition and we had a hard time getting away."

"Not a problem. Since we also worked hard today, I let everyone have some time off. I located some photos you might want to go through, and I placed them in a gallery for you. Let's go to the presentation room and have a look."

Balarie remembered seeing this room earlier. This is where they sold photos to the want-to-be models. "If I can pull off what I think I can, you're going to be very busy. I'll need many new male models to fill this demand."

"I'll do my part. How was the competition today?"

"It was an eye opener. I'm sure there's a demand for models with a certain kind of look, but I want to prove to Mr. Conseco we don't need to forget this other market also."

"I agree. Let's take a look and you tell me what you think. I know many of them."

"I do have one more problem. I need to buy a dress for a tango party on Saturday night."

He laughed like a kid going to his first baseball game. "Don't tell me you're going dancing with Conseco?"

She felt a sudden surge of embarrassment as she wished she hadn't said a word. "Is dancing with him a bad thing?"

"No, I'm sorry. Have you seen him dance?"

"No, but I understand he's good."

"He's better than good and his friends

are better than he is. All of them are professionals. It will be one hell of a night."

"How do you know this?"

"Oh, I'll be at the dance with my camera in hand. Part of my duties as photographer is to document certain events." He paused and turned serious. "The ladies who go to these are dressed . . . humm, to be showy. I think I know a solution. If you'll allow me to make a call, I think I can help. You're so going to owe me for this."

While she wasn't sure what he had in mind, she knew she needed his help.

"Lenny, this is Ethan. I have something for you, if you're . . . interested. Conseco has invited a new girl coming to work for us, Balarie, to go to a tango dance on Saturday night, and I'm afraid she doesn't have a thing to wear." A long pause. "No, if you're busy I can find someone else to design her one."

Another long pause. "Wait and I'll ask her." He offered her a wink. "Do you have some time to go by his shop in a few hours? He needs to take some measurements."

"Sure." She leaned forward. "What's this going to cost me, I can't afford a designer to make me a dress."

Ethan rolled his eyes, much like a

professional actor would. "I'm sure not a penny. I'm going to have to teach you a thing or two on how to get what you want."

Ethan returned to the phone. "I'm taking some photos of her now for her own portfolio. Perhaps I can do some more of her before the dance. You do know that I'll photograph your new design as well."

As she twisted in discomfort, he gave a big thumps up.

"This may be the big chance you've been waiting on, so do me proud."

Ethan snapped the phone shut and returned his attention to Balarie. "Like I said, I have already e-mailed all of these to you. Take some time later tonight to tell me which ones you think will work best. If I'm going to take some experimental shots of you, we need to hurry. Since I have no one helping me with the lights, we'll have to do the best we can, and this is to just do some playing around. Does my idea sound good?"

"Sure. What do I have to lose?"

"There's also one reason I want to do this for you. I want you to see what I put the models though when they come to me. I know you have some experience and this will let me see how much."

"Now the truth comes out." She walked to the set. "I'm not dressed or made up for this, so what are you planning?"

"An exercise of such. I want to name an emotion and see how long it takes you to strike it."

"The session sounds like a doable exercise." Balarie glanced around the set. "I still have no props or clothes to use."

"Such is not a problem, and part of the exercise." He walked closer to her. "I want to capture your face only. It would help for you to lower your top and allow your throat and neck to show."

She understood where he was going. She saw no problem in lowering her blouse for the shoot. "I think I know what you're looking for. For a last minute project, this could be fun."

For the next hour he asked her to distort her face in one emotion after another. He brought out a side of her she didn't know she had. Oh god! What would they look like? The time flew until they finally stopped.

"I know you have an appointment, but I've been thinking. A fast lesson might help you. How long ago has it been since you danced tango and was it Argentina style?" Ethan tossed the camera on the table beside him.

"I did learn Argentina style, but it's been a while. I hope it will come back to me."

"I understand. I'll call you tomorrow if I can arrange anything for you." He wrote an address on a piece of paper. "You should hurry."

###

Tommy descended the stairs to the lower floor. Joe had mentioned Balarie had disappeared to the photography department a few hours ago. She moved almost as fast as he did. "Hello, Ethan. How is it going today?"

"It was another long day, but I'm finishing now."

"I heard Balarie was heading this way. Have you seen her?" The studio seemed so strange with all of the crew gone.

"Yes. She came by to look at some photos of some of the students in the school. I sent them to her in an e-mail and she has them now. I also did some test shots of her. She has a unique photogenic quality."

"She modeled some, but I thought she was giving it up."

"I think all models think they might do some later in life. Anyway, I'm sure she can use it in her current job also. She'll need some publicity shots."

Tommy moved closer to the viewing room. "I don't have but a minute, but I'm interested in seeing what you managed to capture."

A big grin passed Ethan's lips. "I thought you might." He loaded the files and started a presentation run.

The photos of Balarie revealed a raw sexy image he had attempted to avoid for several days. The head shots ventured low to her breasts, but never exposed them. Tommy wondered if she posed nude and Ethan adjusted the lens, or if she kept a halter top on. In any case, they radiated a mixture of pure innocence, capturing the girl next door quality, to the raving sex goddess which drove his business.

Above it all, he saw what Ethan had been working on—emotions. Each shot captured a different look, a different insight to someone he still had not totally figured out, but wanted to explore. "As always, you did an incredible job. It looks like to me she still has a lot of ability to make money as a model."

"Honestly, I thought the same thing. But . . . you never know what makes a model leave the industry. Or . . . in her case, decide to attack it from a different angle." Ethan closed the file. "She had to run a few minutes ago. She told me she needed to find a dress for the tango party."

"I think the late invitation is my fault. It

was a spur of the moment offer. I keep forgetting she's new and not aware of all the going on here. Please send me a copy of these photos also."

Tommy turned to return to his office, knowing fully that he wanted to study these photos again. He also wanted to dig more into her modeling career. He knew of at least one person he could talk to and receive some answers.

Chapter 13

Balarie entered the designer world she loved to explore as Lenny Askew dropped a golden cloth he was measuring and rushed over to her. He waved at two assistants to join him. "We've some major work ahead of us. I know Conseco will be dressed to show off his abilities. You do know he's an extremely good tango dancer, don't you?"

"I've been told. I also told him I could dance, but not professionally. I'm sure he'll have many chances to dance with others. He said this group had many great dancers in it."

"Okay, girlie. The dancing will be all on you, but my job is to make you the most beautiful peacock there. Damn! This has to fit like a glove since you have a great body for dancing. However, I do need to know how much you can bend. I sure don't want the fabric to rip while you dance. So, to start with, how much leg extension can you do?"

Balarie remembered practicing dance in

school before. "I can kick over my head, but not in these clothes."

"I see, we can allow for full movement." He raised his fingers and snapped them, sending the two girls helping him into motion. "I need measurements and my drawing board."

The girls helped her to remove all but the essentials as they measured every part of her body—twice.

"I have dancing shoes already being designed for me." She hoped they would do.

"Drop them by tomorrow morning and I'll check them out." Andrew lowered his head again and kept drawing. His hands moved like lightening as he sketched with the flair of a symphony conductor.

She redressed as he continued with the girls huddled around him. The short exchanges meant nothing to her as they passed comments on the design. Having a minute to think, she glanced around the shop to study the various designs he had in progress. To be able to create something from an idea impressed her. Being able to do so in two days would be a miracle.

Thirty minutes later he waved for her to join him. "I have three versions of what might work. Tell me what you think?"

The stunning detail of the first one

stopped her breathing. He had definitely missed his calling as a painter. "Wow! I can't believe you're so talented in sketching."

"Thanks, but I'm working on the dress and not painting. Tell me what you think about wearing this one."

"I would love it." She looked at the next two. Both were to die for. "I don't know how to select one over the other. You'll have to choose the best for me."

"In that case, it will have to be this one. We'll start with glittering red, almost metallic polyester knit which I'll stretch a delicate black lace over. And, of course, have it highlighted with sequin and beaded appliqués. In contrast, the sleeve will be further accented with a red mesh detailed to reflect variations of red as it flows and extends to the loop for the finger. Perhaps a soft pleated trim in a layered red satin or chiffon would be perfect. I'll work on perfecting my thoughts later. I want to ensure a dramatic open back in the shape of a heart accented with rhinestones which we will extend to the hip. This full dress design will help to give you more curve appeal."

"Is that a good way to tell me I have a flat butt?"

He blinked and continued to describe his

creation, which she could tell he was changing every minute. "Yes, but with a ruffled fullness in the skirt, I think a dramatic opening could highlight your legs. I want to create something elegant in one moment and feisty as hell the next. However, it will be your skills as a dancer that will bring it to life."

"I don't know how to thank you for this."

"This is one time that I hope I'm the one who owes you. Come back tomorrow night for a fitting. Shall we say the same time? We'll have it ready by Saturday night, and if you'll allow me, I want your makeup to match the dress, so I'll provide a stylist here for you."

"You're doing too much."

"In this business, nothing is . . . too much. Now rush along and see if you can find some fast tango lessons somewhere."

Lessons would be nice, but where on such short notice?

###

Tommy pushed himself harder than normal as he pounded out the miles on his exercise bike. The images of Balarie invaded his thoughts as he imagined making love to her. He had studied her photos for hours until he decided to work out again. This was much too late for him, but he needed to do something to distract his mind. Instead, this only allowed him to dig deeper into his needs, and ones which have gone unattended for a long time.

He kept telling himself he had to have the legs for Saturday night. Tomorrow night he would have private lessons to sharpen his skills. With many of the ladies attending known to be very talented dancers, he needed to be at his peak. He felt curious to see how his friends would react to him bringing Balarie. He felt sure they would be nice to her and help her learn tango the correct way—the Argentina way.

He heard a door open behind him. One of the housekeepers walked in. "Oops, I'm sorry, Mr. Conseco. I didn't know you would be working out this late."

Annoyed, he stopped the bike, as the interruption in his rhythm effectively ended his concentration. His legs had reached their max anyway. "No, it's alright. I'm finishing now."

"I can come back later. I wanted to clean the room before I went to bed." She looked small and much too dainty to do much, but she always managed to keep his place clean without ever getting in the way.

He paused to study her body which was lean and trim, and with the freshness of youth of a girl in her late twenties. She lived in a room on the other side of his personal area along with Peter, who also maintained his condo. The ten thousand square feet condo needed constant attention.

"Maria, I probably don't ever say it, but I do appreciate you working for me. Everything is always perfect."

Tommy watched her smile radiate. "Thank you, Mr. Conseco." She quickly lowered her eyes to keep from making contact with his.

He never fully understood why people acted afraid of him so much. He felt like he was a nice guy, and he never acted physical, or yelled at people. The images of what people thought about him concerned him, as it often did, but it had been the way

he had pushed himself to be the best. He expected the same from his effort and admired those who also gave it their ultimate effort. For some it came easier than others. Some struggled so hard but missed the mark. Others made it appear so easy their work often went unnoticed, much like Maria's chores.

He realized this one unimposing girl had taught him something he had not noticed for years. The wall he built around him also sealed his heart inside a coffin of doom. He would soon be forty. Is this the way his life would be lived out?

Maria's eyes twinkled with such a flare of happiness in them his decision made him feel good. "How long have you been working for me, Maria?"

"I think almost five years now, Mr. Conseco."

He didn't realize she had worked for him for so long. "Yes, time does go fast. If there is anything I can do for you, let me know."

Her eyes watered slightly as she made contact with his. "There's only one thing I would love to do."

Feeling generous, he waited for her request.

"I have family in Italy I haven't seen since I came to America. It would be so good to see them."

Tommy realized the money she made didn't allow her to make international trips. "Have any of your family been to America?"

"I'm not sure I can arrange it, they have lives there."

"Well, perhaps you should go see them."

He watched her face flush. "I wish."

Tommy walked closer and placed a hand on her shoulder. "Let me see what I can do." He owed her something special.

He knew it would make him feel good to help, perhaps much better than her.

"Thank you." She flashed one last demure smile and glanced at the room. "I like cleaning this room."

Tommy watched her walk away from him. Her firm rear attracted his attention, but no. He felt sure she would accommodate him and relieve his sexual frustration, never to say a word. Still, it would be wrong.

The time had come for him to allow someone in his life, someone who he wouldn't feel that he had to hide his feelings from. An outstanding body would be fantastic, but he wanted so much more.

He yelled over his shoulder. "I'm going to the media room, and would love some tea to relax."

"Yes, sir. I'll bring you some of your favorite green herbal tea in a minute."

###

Balarie reflected on her lessons. She didn't admit to all of them or the cost of ballroom dancing lessons which extended for over two years. Tango consisted of only a small part of her lessons. She had also been around long enough to know the difference between American style and Argentina style. It was huge.

Balarie slipped in the first disc, the first of five that she had rented from the video store a few minutes earlier. She would use the internet later to find something for Friday night. She read the cover describing the Argentina tango which blasted the American style that the famous dance instructor, Arthur Murray, had developed to teach to his students. He had wanted a system easily teachable by his studios. Argentina is much more freestyle and dynamic, pushing the flare to extremes often.

Balarie remembered the words of her instructor of spelling out the words T . . . a . . . n . . . g . . . o in a rhythm of slow, slow, quick, quick, slow. As she read she recognized the word staccato, a word meaning to strike the floor quickly with your foot and avoiding the shuffling or dragging of her feet. To add flare, the only exception was the final slow count of the pattern, allowing her to slowly drag in her free foot.

Balarie cleared a small space to practice. It would have to do. She really needed room to travel or walk around the room. The bulk of the first lesson was walking, but this was what she remembered from her lessons.

The CD went through the basic steps

over and over. She knew this part. She needed much more advanced lessons. As she started to remove the CD and move on to the next she discovered a surprise—a special performance of a national championship. Now this is what she wanted to study.

As the couple addressed each other, the female dancer wrapped her left elbow around her partner's right elbow and

adjusted her left thumb under his right tricep. With an elegant flare, she raised her right hand for her partner to hold at about eye level. Her smooth arched back pressed her body forward, joining her to him from the ribcage to the hips. With her connection slightly to the right, it looked like the dancer had positioned her crotch directly on his hip. Images of dancing with Tommy invaded her mind. How was she to maintain a straight face? She needed to work with him later, damn it.

As the dance proceeded, she forced her mind to remember the flow and the steps. It was much too fast and impossible to learn overnight. She needed steps she could learn. More importantly, she needed to know the basics and not really screw up on them. It was going to be a long night.

###

Tommy shuffled through the media data

banks as he relaxed and curled back in his favorite lazy boy type chair. The personalized full wall screen allowed him the ability to examine any flaws or distractions needing to be corrected.

He found the files he wanted in his e-mail account—the ones Ethan had promised him of Balarie. As he flipped through them one by one, he soon appreciated Ethan's work more than usual. He had captured much more than beauty; he had isolated a series of personalities transcending the arena of modeling. Many times buyers ask for a certain look, a special radiance they couldn't explain, but knew it when they saw it.

The low cut shots, the ones barely above her breast, gave strong illusions to her being totally naked. However, he assumed better. Still, he knew she wasn't shy. He remembered her stripping to her panties and bra without much hesitation, a time it took extreme willpower to avoid staring at her.

One photo where she blew him a soft, gentle kiss dominated his attention. He couldn't help from wanting to return the favor. When he reached the end of the session, he restarted from the beginning where he fully intended to memorize each in much more detail this time.

He heard the door creek open behind him as Maria entered the room. "I prepared your tea, sir."

"Thank you." She startled him as he felt like a kid being caught watching porno. Why did he have such feelings? This was his job. Suddenly he realized why—this time it was personal. This image belonged to a real person, and one he wanted to know better.

Chapter 14

Balarie flopped into a chair at the dance studio. The upcoming tango dance wasn't exactly a date, so why did she feel so nervous? In fact, Tommy wasn't even picking her up. However, she knew he had invited her, and she would be both dancing with him and introduced to his friends. This dance felt about as close to a date as he apparently would allow.

Balarie swallowed some water to help quench the thirst created by the last hour of dancing. This last minute dance lesson made her feel completely like an idiot. Who was she fooling? She couldn't learn to dance this fast. She needed to sit on the sideline and watch the professionals.

Again, she looked forward to learning more about the dance tonight. Tommy said they were nice people and loved to teach the dance to others. This time she needed to take it one step at a time—funny how she put it that way.

Her instructor returned. "We have another thirty minutes if you can make it."

"I don't think I have any choice." She struggled to her feet and walked to the center of the floor.

"You have one advantage. The man's job is to make you look good. It's his responsibility to lead you through the steps, and to present you to the crowds."

"Yes, but I have to learn to follow his instructions."

"Let's work some more on technique. I think it will be nice for you to concentrate on the basic tango relationship. More than anything else, it's a walk, a time to connect with each other. Unlike many dances, in tango you want to hang onto your partner. Your right hand isn't resting around his back, but it's digging into his arm muscle here. Your left hand's firmly attached to his, including a slight wrapping around his forearm. But most importantly, you're connected together."

"This could be a little uncomfortable."

He smiled and pulled her closer. "Tonight when you dance, think of the culture which created the dance and live it, own it. If you think like most American women you'll never learn the Argentina style. It'll show."

"But I am an American."

"You asked me to teach you how to dance Argentina style. Watch the others, leave your inhibitions at home tonight, and have a good time."

Balarie stepped closer. "I can't see my shoes, or how to walk."

"Your concentration should be directly above your left hand. I know how you will feel lost on the floor, and walking backwards is something requiring a lot of trust. But remember that it's your partner's responsibility to move you around the floor. He'll direct the way you travel. You need to learn to trust him."

"Okay, I only have time to practice one or two dips."

"Now you're asking for the impossible." He stepped from her and shook his head.

"I remember a few from before. Please help me have something in my arsenal."

"Okay, allow me to teach you one and we'll try it. If you can master it in a few minutes I have a small variation you can try. But remember maintaining *el ritmo*, the rhythm is more important than a fancy dip."

"Let's do it."

###

Next stop—Lenny's design studio. Balarie hoped for the best. She saw a partial of it last night and it looked amazing. She knew they had a lot of work to do to finish it. She wandered to the back of the shop, looking for someone. An assistant saw her and rushed over. "Good, we don't have much time to waste. I'm going to be helping you with your hair and makeup. A professional will be here to add the final touches. "

"Where is Lenny?"

"He didn't like part of the red mesh he selected and dashed off for a different one."

"He's making a change this late?"

"Don't worry. He has worked many fashion shows and knows how to work under pressure. I need to slick your hair back and tie it in a knot."

Balarie had assumed they may want to do this, but with her curly hair this wouldn't be easy.

"Are you sure this will work?"

"I'm sure. Relax."

Balarie allowed the girl to try, but it wouldn't relax, much like what she thought. When Lenny walked in he noticed it immediately. "I have a plan." He opened the bag he carried under an arm. "Yes, this will do perfectly."

Balarie followed his lead to the center of the studio. "If I did my work properly this will fit like a glove. Let's get you in it and see if I have to make any last minute changes."

Balarie stripped down and wiggled into

it—perfect. She squealed. "I love it! I feel like I'm dancing with almost nothing on."

"Good! I need to add a few accessories. So, if you'll give me a minute." He worked on her wrist to add a flared cloth as he motioned for her to move to the makeup chair again. "Michelle will be here in a minute. I want the lip stick as red as the outfit, and oh yes, the eyes as smoky as possible. While they're doing that, I'll add one last touch." He hurried off with a piece of the mesh.

Michelle soon walked in and went to work on her face. Balarie knew to say nothing and wait on the look to materialize. The artist was good. After she finished, Lenny rushed over to her. "Allow me to add this." He attached a layered hat made of the red mesh to cover her misbehaving hair.

"I assume you have your dancing shoes with you."

"Yes, in my bag."

"Good, I want to see the full effect."

As Balarie walked over to slip them on, Lenny studied her accessories. "Do you have a clutch purse to match this?"

"Oops, not with me."

"Not a problem. I'll loan you one." He motioned for his assistant to find one, as he turned his head to an angle. "I think we're ready. Tell Ethan I want top notch photos of this."

"I'll see to it you get some good ones." She leaned over and offered him a cheek press while kissing the air beside him and avoiding the smudge of her lipstick. "Thank you."

Chapter 15

Tommy studied his solid black dancing outfit, highlighted with a red handkerchief and slim red tie which helped to accentuate his height. His shoes felt firm and tight enough to support his movements. He had looked forward to this night for a long time. These friends lived and breathed tango—Argentina styled tango.

After entering the dance hall, he glanced around, and wondered if Balarie had arrived yet. She was the one girl that he wanted to see and dance with. The confidence he had in his dancing ability made him feel somewhat cocky, but he wanted to impress her, maybe more so than any other girl he would be dancing with. He didn't expect her to be too skilled, but fun to be with.

He saw several models from his agency along the sides. Several could tango some and would make great photos later. He knew he could count on Ethan to make everyone stand out.

After passing by one old friend to

another, Tommy suddenly watched a dress drift across the floor. The style captured his attention. Someone had gone all out to impress the others. The elegant heart shape cut away in the back surrounded with gemstones set the mood for a dress meant to flow. The red mesh hairpiece holding dark, blonde hair offered a perfect compliment. He wondered who designed the dress. He knew he would find out soon enough as he ventured closer.

As she turned, he came face to face with brilliant blue eyes set apart by the smoky highlight, blotting out everything else around her. Tommy knew these eyes, but being stunned in the setting, he froze. The dazzling red lipstick also bewildered his ability to control his emotions. Balarie looked absolutely beautiful.

"Wow, you look impressive tonight. I have many people to introduce you to, but with the way you look I'm tempted to hide you away and save you strictly for myself."

Balarie stepped back slightly and studied his clothing. "You know, I could say the same about you, and you know how flattery . . . will get you everything."

"Promise?" Remarkable, he meant the compliment to be sincere, but she probably accepted it as verbosity at its worst. With many people crowding around them, perhaps she acted like

the smart one. He saw no sense in starting more rumors that he needed to deal with. They had already taken their photo together several times lately and publicized them in the media.

"I've been hearing everyone say what a good dancer you are. You have an amazing reputation." Balarie shuffled to the side to scan the room. "I don't think I know anyone here, but since I haven't danced tango in a long time, I think it's understandable. You said these were your friends."

"Yes, I've danced with many of these ladies before. I'll introduce you to many people tonight." A flash caught him off guard. He turned to see Ethan smiling over the top of his camera.

"Turn toward me." Ethan continued to motion to them to comply. "The two of you look absolutely stunning tonight."

"Yes. I'll agree Balarie is possibly going to capture the dance tonight. I was hoping to dance with her, but I may have to stand in line."

"Oh, I'm sure she'll save you at least a dance or two. Capturing the emotions of the dance will be the photos I really want to nail." Ethan motioned to others he wanted to catch as he left them alone.

Tommy backed away to take a better look at her dress. "I don't think I've ever seen anything exactly like this before."

"There's not one *exactly* like it anywhere. Lenny Askew designed it for me specifically for this dance."

"Impressive, and an original. How did you mange to pull off such a pleasant surprise so quickly?"

"Lucky, just pure lucky. And, I'll admit it required a lot of fast work to have it all completed in time."

Tommy watched his friend, Antonio Fario walk to the center of the dance floor and lift his hands high to obtain everyone's attention. The sooner they started dancing the better since he bored often with people making aimless chatter. And tonight, he wanted to dance with Balarie more than anyone he had ever danced with before. His dreams from the night before filled his mind with thoughts of tonight's prospective pleasure.

The crowd accommodated the speaker's wishes and quickly departed from the center of the floor. "Hello my friends and tango lovers. We have an incredible night planned for everyone! First, I would like to thank those responsible for such a line up. I'm sure everyone here knows Thomas Conseco and how much he loves the tango. And, by the way, have you noticed the girl with him? I can't wait to watch them dance, can you?" He lifted his arms for applause.

"Thank you." Tommy raised one hand to wave at those around him, while he internally wished Antonio hadn't announced it like that. He knew the spotlight would be on them later, and he still wasn't sure exactly how much Balarie could dance. He needed to find out quietly before they were expected to dance in the center of the room. The practice session, including the line exercise, would let him know.

Antonio regained control after several models, which included Marian and Linda, passed closer to Tommy to offer a special thank you. "Next, I want to introduce you to your band for the night." He pointed to the far side of the room, where the group played a quick sampling of things to come. "I'll let the Marco Vanzella band leader, Marco himself, introduce his band members in a minute."

Marco offered a brief wave to the crowd.

"We have some of the best dancers from Argentina with us tonight, and who will be delighting us with some special performances. As always, they'll be dancing with others, and offering insights on how to improve our own dancing. I highly encourage you to avail yourself of this unbelievable opportunity."

Tommy contemplated the dances he would encounter tonight, but most of all the dances Balarie would be accepting. He had no hold on her, but he hated to see her dancing with other men. The same thoughts haunted him the night before when he studied her photos. For once in his life he wanted a woman reserved only to him, and someone sheltered from the rest of the world. He hated to share her. This was a strange feeling he had trouble understanding.

After glancing around the room, Tommy watched many of the guys passing glances at Balarie. These guys knew he would become distracted soon, thus leaving her to their mercy. He needed to make plans, or watch her dance with others all night, but how?

While developing his plan, Antonio continued, as he pointed to his left. "Please join me as we enjoy our first demonstration of exactly what it means to dance tango—Argentina style. I give you Myra and her husband Pedro Sanchez."

As they stepped to the center of the floor, the crowd cleared more room for them, and thus emptied the entire hardwood dancing section. While waiting for the music to start, they addressed each other in an *apilado*, a standard embrace which dramatically froze the attention of the crowd.

In the moment, Tommy stood next to Balarie and fought the unmistaken urge to hold her hand. The back of her hand rested against his. Should he?

The music started and he lost his chance as the applause erupted. Balarie maintained her hands close to her side as she appeared to focus on the dance. He, instead, concentrated on her smile. As the dance advanced, he turned to follow the steps which he knew and wished he could teach Balarie.

Balarie's personality radiated through her excitement in watching them dance. Her intense study of the movements indicated a true passion for dance. Tommy knew this wouldn't be the last time they stepped on a dance floor, and the next time they would have practiced together. He wanted to present her to the crowd, and in the way the dance was intended to be performed.

As expected, as soon as they finished, the band went immediately into a practice rhythm where the group formed a long line to travel around the room. Would Balarie know how to do this?

With all eyes on him, Tommy stepped in line and felt Balarie behind him. He allowed the music to flow through him. He knew she would be in his arms before the night ended. Hopefully she would follow his steps, *el caminar,* as they practiced the basic movements.

After once around the floor, he recognized the restless nature of the dancers who broke away from the established line. He turned to face Balarie, but she had disappeared. Another guy had grabbed her first dance. He tried to hide his disappointment, but wasn't allowed much time to pout about it since several models rushed to him for a chance to dance. While enduring the onslaught, he noticed other ladies who nodded him a *cabeceo,* an invitation to dance, from across the room.

###

The dress, the makeup, and most importantly the music made Balarie feel confident. Still, she felt best in downplaying her ability to dance and let the guys teach her. Her first suitor offered charm and charisma in the way he danced patiently with her while offering slow small movements and instructions as she followed his lead. Without a doubt, he worked as a tango instructor somewhere.

With the crowd dancing around her, she lost all sight of Tommy. With his height and hers, she would have thought that he would be easy to spot. As the first dance ended, her partner passed her on to the next guy, but only after he attempted to introduced himself. She knew it was bad of her, but the name didn't register.

Two dances later she had only briefly spotted Tommy on the floor. Could he have been attacked as quickly as she was? She really didn't need to answer her own question. The real question was how to vacate the floor and find a drink.

A quick change in tempo allowed her the chance to escape as she fanned her chest. "I need to take a small break."

"Please allow me to find you a drink." Her last partner acted as if he wanted to get to know her better.

"Maybe later, I need to go to the ladies area, but I'll be back soon." She needed time to rest and not become attached to one guy or the other. As she left the floor, she anticipated coming under attack again. The benefits or cost of dressing to impress made her a target.

In the ladies room, Balarie watched the other women studying her dress, and wanting to know all of the details. As she told what she wore, she watched the women making notes. Then the much anticipated question of where can they buy such a dress. She had no answer, but agreed to provide the information if they would e-mail her. She reached for her small clutch and located a few business cards.

As she walked from the ladies room she giggled. She knew that Lenny had a hit on his hands. She needed to work more with him to expand his market.

After arriving at a small bar near a resting area, she saw Tommy who was surrounded by models from the agency. He acted polite and dignified, but bored. Perhaps he was the one needing rescuing. The models stared at her as she joined them. Their jealous messages radiating from their stances shifted only so slightly.

"You disappeared on me." When her eyes locked in on his, the rest of the room vanished.

She watched him focus on the dress she wore. "Such a dress is made to flow. I think it's time to find out what you know."

"It will be your job to make it happen on the dance floor since I have no reputation to defend. But now, we'll see if you live up to yours." She waited for his reaction to the challenge.

Tommy turned to one of the models

beside him. "Find Ethan, I don't think he wants to miss this." Tommy turned toward Balarie and offered his arm, acting like the perfect gentleman as long as he stood in front of the crowd, but then again, he always acted this way.

All eyes seemed to focus on them. While he acted accustomed to being in the spot light, she struggled to contain her fear. As far as she could tell, however, no other woman held his interest. Tommy could make her career skyrocket. Pushing the boundaries of their newly formed relationship felt risky, but at this point, what did she have to lose?

Tommy paraded her to a starting point on the floor and paused. She watched side glances and covert conversations abound. She felt him take her hand in his. Was it a show of affection or encouragement?

As his appearance on the floor spread, the crowd thinned. A knot hit her stomach. Would he be flamboyant, or gentle and caring about her abilities? What a time to find out.

Tommy leaned closer to her. "I'll walk with you to start, since there's no reason to hurry. After I give you room to freelance, I'll understand better just how much you know."

A lump went to her throat as he put on

notice that she would soon be under the spotlight.

The music soon stopped, as the band waited for them to get in position, *el salida*. She locked her arm around his and squeezed his muscular tricep, affixing her place next to him. She pressed her hip deep into his side as her ribcage melted into his, effectively bonding their bodies into one.

With her left hand floating to his, the connection would be complete. Well almost. She raised her right knee in an *enganche*, rubbing his side with the deadly accuracy of a cobra prepared to strike. The slit in the side of the dress performed as designed as she witnessed the first flash. A low moan coming from the crowd verified their pleasure in seeing her long slim leg exposed.

Balarie turned her face toward Tommy, as his masculine jaw demanded attention. He showed no teeth, only a strong determination to focus on the dance. In studying him, she concentrated on his lips which were strong, solid, and above all else—desirable. Frozen in time, she waited for the band to start.

On the first note, Tommy turned his face sharply to his right—Balarie matched him by making a quick turn to her left. She listened for the beat and concentrated. She was now fully in his hands. She needed to follow the slightest command he offered her.

Slow, slow, quick, quick, slow— Tommy jerked his body around to face her. She left stepped between his knees and extended her right leg behind her, arching her back as she dropped near the floor, holding it for a full beat. He lifted her gracefully, powerfully, as he maintained control. The crowd clapped as her dress returned to cover her leg.

Balarie slithered like a snake climbing a tree, caressing him with her leg until her body reunited with his. Her emotionless face inched closer and was now only inches from lips she wanted to devour.

When Tommy jerked his head and body to his right this time, Balarie reversed and shifted to her right displaying a rift in their emotions, an *amague* used to embellish her own style. However, she followed his lead and glided *atras* while counting slow, slow, quick, quick, slow in this backward movement. After forcing her

close to him, he kicked several times between her feet and planted his weight before releasing her hold, and allowing her to freestyle—her moment.

Balarie swirled away from him and started to walk gingerly, but purposefully defiant. She felt him grab her hand and reunite her to him with his face inches from her own. She could feel him breathe while she envisioned the passion escaping through his eyes. She wanted him, now, later, it didn't matter—she wanted him.

Again they walked, as Balarie waited for Tommy's direction. He surprised her and dragged her slightly off the floor with her toe grazing the wooden floor. She wrapped both arms around his neck and waited for a lift. He didn't disappoint her and swirled her to the left, but released her long enough to finish one on her own. Before she could rest, he pulled her into an inside swirl and back into his arms where she wrapped her leg around his again. The flow of the dress highlighted every move, exactly as the designer had hoped.

As the last movement ended, she lowered her head to his shoulder in a display of submission. The crowd yelled and even expressed a few whistles. Her heart beat fast, not because of the exertion, but because of the powerful effect Tommy had on her. Did he feel it also?

With the crowd pressing tightly around them, she felt it tear her heart as he released her. Their time together ended for now, as the other dancers separated them with congratulations and praise. But the last parting glance from Tommy answered her one question. It embraced much more than a dance.

###

Tommy flexed his back and greeted one person after another as he walked off the dance floor. How did Balarie learn to dance so professionally? She was no beginner. He wanted to know her back story, and since everyone had one, he yearned to know hers.

An instructor he used years ago approached him. "You're doing astoundingly well, and it never hurts to have a beautiful woman dancing with you. I'm almost embarrassed to dance with you after a demonstration like that. But, it doesn't surprise me you would bring in a ringer."

A sudden rush of pride filled his chest as he looked for Balarie. However, he knew she would be fighting off every guy at the dance for a long time. He cleared his head long enough to see his instructor staring at him, and waiting on a dance. "Sorry, I'll be glad to dance with you."

While Tommy needed to offer his best in dancing with her, he found himself looking for Balarie. Where was she? Who was she dancing with?

After making the turn in the corner, Tommy saw Balarie on the far side of the floor, stretching forward, revealing one leg up to her hip. He needed to concentrate on his own dance as he blinked from another flash startling him.

The thoughts of Balarie's body firmly placed next to his aroused his inner feelings and a sexual desire he tried so hard to suppress, not to mention a sudden rise in his manhood that he hope no one would notice. His pants were tight, too tight for such a reaction.

An hour passed, then two. He danced with many girls, normally the highlight of the night, but nothing compared to Balarie. He wanted at least one more dance. He needed to drink something. The workout had drained him of fluids. He thanked the last girl, Marian who worked for him and walked to the side bar.

He located Balarie's dress in front of the bar ahead of him, how could he forget it? He paused as he waited on her to turn.

"Hi, I wondered if we would see each other again tonight."

"I think you can count on at least one more dance. I have to ask—how did you learn to dance so well?"

"Oh, I rented a video on it—why, was I like really bad?"

"I think you know better and I'm extremely impressed. Humm, that had to be one hell of a video. I'm having several people join me on my boat later for an after party. I'd love for you to join us." He felt like a high school boy asking a girl for a date.

"It's kind of late notice, don't you think?"

"Yes, I should've mentioned it earlier, but I totally forgot. I do want to see you more tonight and hear where you learned to dance so nice. So please join me. I have room in the limo and I'll make sure you're taken care of."

"You know if we keep doing this we'll start rumors. Is that what you want to deal with?"

She was right. However, she did work with him and it could be explained. He also knew of other after parties, ones she would be invited to if he didn't move fast. "I'll assure you my boat is private and we can relax. So please come."

"Since you said please, I think it would be nice to relax. Now . . . can I have the last dance with you?"

A tingling sensation rushed along his back and entered his neck before reaching a crescendo in his scalp. "It would be my honor." Forget the damn drink, he wanted her in his arms and her face locked in front of his.

Upon stepping on the floor, he watched the reactions from the other dancers. She planted her body next to his and eased into character which excited him with a desire he forced himself to hide—for now.

She offered many moves he hadn't seen before. Where did she learn tango like that? She pulled from him and it felt like a part of his flesh torn from his body. She returned and intensified her attention on him. The sight of her dark smoky eye shadow shut out the worries of the world as her brilliant blue eyes impregnated his heart.

He held a complete count, which created a dramatic moment in time before her leg wrapped around his leg, and added to his pleasure. The grazing rub of her slow methodic seduction left him struggling to recover. He had to—he did have a lot of eyes watching him, and a reputation to maintain. No woman had ever penetrated his walls before, but then again, he hadn't wanted sex with anyone more than he did with her—right now.

As the dance ended, she collapsed in his arms and gazed into his eyes which were now inches away, but yet so far. His focus shifted to her lips which were so damn beautiful, and so inviting.

Flashes brought him out of the trance

and not a moment too soon. One more
second and he would have full knowledge
of her lips and more. He allowed her to part
from him, but held her hand, and a soft
connection to the future.

Chapter 16

Balarie slid to the far side of the limo and made room for the others, which included Antonio, who organized the dance, his wife Marcie, and the two models, Marian and Linda, who were obviously selected for the night to make Tommy look good.

Tommy settled into the seat next to Balarie. "Thanks for coming. I wanted to reach the boat before everyone else to make sure all is in order."

Marian, one of the models, acted bored and cast side glances at Balarie. Her meaning was obvious since she expressed hopes of being in Balarie's place. Balarie remembered how Tommy said he never touched the models. But still, how could any guy resist such temptation? They offered amazing bodies and obviously were eager to do whatever he wanted and more.

As she rested close to Tommy, his presence penetrated her thin outfit, which seemed so wrong for an after party. While she glanced around the limo, she wondered exactly how rich Tommy was. He had some of the top models in the world working for him and his commissions came off the top.

Antonio patted Marcie's knee and motioned to Balarie and Tommy. "That was one hell of a dance tonight. I think your performance made the attendees glad they came. I don't think I've seen so much emotion in a dance for a long time."

"Thank you. It was fun to finally dance with Mr. Conseco."

"I think you have to be kidding me since you look like you've danced together for years. I've judged dancing competitions for a long time, and I can tell you the one element sealing a win is the connection. Tonight, it looked incredible. You make a great couple."

Balarie felt the rush of blood to her face, and she didn't often blush. "I had a great partner."

"In any case, I want to see the photos when they're available."

Balarie noticed a smile from Marian whom took her role seriously of playing a bimbo, but something made Balarie think that she might be much smarter than she appeared. She could see the wheels turning in Marian's mind. She came on these events to be seen and if someone like

Balarie could help her, so

be it. She had to admire the girl for wanting a career so bad to do whatever it took.

Tommy broke the silence. "I think a quick bottle of bubbly would be in order." He reached for a center console and retrieved a bottle specifically planned for the event. Linda, the model next to him, handed out the glasses to everyone. She must have been in the limo before to know where they were.

As Balarie watched the glasses being filled, she wondered what the toast would be. A feeling of wealth, of power surrounded her as she explored the possibilities. She felt like she was on a roll. Would it last?

###

Tommy walked ahead of the group and waved at Michael Richards, the manager on his boat. He retained no captain, why should he? He hardly ever took it out to sea. It did represent the perfect place to host parties. One day he would make a long voyage in it, but he had been making himself this promise for a long time. He knew this size yacht had a range to easily make it to Europe, and it was the chosen destination when he bought it several years ago.

"I think we have it all arranged for you on top, sir." Michael sprang into action and summoned a crew to service the event. "I located a small band you had requested to play some relaxing music for you, but they also know some tango selections just in case, like you mentioned."

Tommy patted Michael on the shoulder as he passed by him. "I knew I could count on you."

The night proceeded much like Tommy had planned, but with a small added benefit. Balarie was with him, and he now wanted to know more about her. Later tonight he planned to ask her many questions.

After climbing the stairs to the upper deck, he surveyed the party area outlined in small, white, Christmas-like lights. The decorative wooden panels glistened in the sparkling array. The cool breeze bringing with it the salty smell he loved blew in from the Atlantic and added the perfect weather to relax from the night of dancing.

Tommy turned to his guest. "Make yourself at home and order a drink of whatever you want. The others will be here soon."

The group lounged around as he walked over to the band adjusting their instruments. "Thank you so much for coming. I heard you play great relaxing music."

After receiving smiles from the band members, Tommy turned back to the group and studied Balarie. He had a few minutes so why not show her around? Since he knew she liked red wine, he walked to the bar. "I need something special tonight in a robust red. What do we have?"

Tommy watched the eyes of the bartender. "I heard one bottle you own is peaking tonight, perhaps it's time to check it out."

"Perfect." A prized wine for a spectacular night excited him. He waited for the guy to go to the wine cellar as he continued to analyze Balarie. The outfit she wore highlighted her best features, especially her face and neck line. Her skin radiated in the mass of small twinkling lights. As she turned directly toward him the dress also emphasized her breasts which were firm and a perfectly proportioned asset she needed as a model. The sudden thought of her modeling diverted his thoughts for a minute back to why did she quit modeling to start working as a booker?

The bartender handed him the two glasses of wine. "Please tell me how it is. It has been exciting in following it here."

Tommy smiled and felt generous. "Pour yourself one and enjoy. I think you'll have much more appreciation than most people here."

"Are you sure, sir?"

"Yes. Please be my guest." Tommy turned and walked toward Balarie. He enjoyed each step as it enhanced his appreciation of her personality, and lit up his evening with prospects for later in the night.

"I have a wine for you that I think you'll enjoy. I've been saving it for over four years. It was, in fact, the first wine I purchased for the cellar on board."

She accepted the glass and studied the wine. "It sounds like you were saving it for something special. So why tonight?"

"The truth is that everyday should be special. My problem, like I assume many people, is that I don't take time to appreciate it."

He lifted his glass to inhale the aromas which were so refreshingly different. As he recognized each, he decided to wait on Balarie to discover them on her own. He swirled his glass as he waited, allowing the scents to heighten.

Balarie closed her eyes for a second which gave him a chance to further study her eye makeup. The artist had worked magic. She opened them to direct her focus back at him in a flashing turn of events, and thus catching him off guard to compete with the intense feelings she displayed.

"I think I smell raspberry and currants. How about you?"

She was better than he thought. He lifted his glass toward her glass and thought of an appropriate toast. "I think we should drink to the tango and to emotions it produces when it's performed with zest."

"I can drink to that."

The time passed quickly as other guest arrived. Tommy needed to bide his time. He needed to think through his actions. Flirting with disaster scared him as he considered an obstacle course he had never attempted before. Still, these uncharted waters intrigued him. Playing it as he ventured forward added to the challenge. He usually got what he wanted—but this time, he wasn't sure what he wanted, exactly. Tommy, however, knew he wouldn't be turning back after he reached a certain point.

###

Balarie enjoyed the quiet, lazy feeling the wine created inside her. She had managed to pull off a dance she could only dream of, as she mentally thanked the instructors who had earlier pushed her into learning them also. She could only imagine the gossip that would be in the high society pages tomorrow morning.

She watched the two models, Linda and Marian, talking off to one side. They looked tired, but maintained their pose, as they were obviously paid to do. An idea floated in her mind as she walked over to them. "How are you holding up?"

Marian's long, blonde hair hanging in delicate curls bounced as she turned to Balarie and nodded toward her in a so-so condition. "I think the night is winding down and will be over soon. I'm so glad tomorrow is Sunday and I'll have some time off to relax."

"I had an idea while I was relaxing a few minutes ago. I'm working on a special assignment I hope to have finalized soon. Both of you have inspired me to try something."

Both girls leaned their heads closer to listen, as they concentrated on her words. "If it's any kind of modeling job with potential, we would definitely be interested."

"This isn't to be discussed anywhere, but I'll let you know I'm working on a major project where the central theme will be . . . dressing your boyfriend for success."

"I love it already!" Marian's deep-blue eyes sparked for the first time tonight as new life seemed to circulate inside her.

Balarie felt relived in knowing they liked her idea. "While it might not seem to be a major part, or the center of attention, I think by using the same models repeatedly, it will have a major impact on someone's career."

"I think I understand. Our job will be to highlight the male model and make him look good."

"Exactly, and much like what you're doing for Tommy tonight."

The two models smiled before turning to each other and exchanging a short high five. "We're in. It sounds like fun. What can we do to help?"

"I might need you to work with Ethan, the agency staff photographer to do a mock up of what I'm proposing."

"Just name when."

"Good. I have your numbers and will be in touch. It may happen soon, like in maybe tomorrow."

"In such a case, we need to see about getting some sleep."

"One more thing—don't tell Tommy about this yet. I want to spring it on him in the meeting on Monday."

Linda leaned closer to Balarie. "Be

careful. He has sent many girls home who didn't follow his rules. He's more than strict. I hope you know what you're doing."

"So far all is good. Don't worry."

"Yes, Conseco appears to like you very much. This is the first time I've seen him take to someone so much. You're a lucky woman."

"Thanks." The compliment made Balarie feel great, but she wanted to be admired for her work and results and not simply for

her personality or whatever else it was he appeared to like. However, she did find his attention flattering as she turned to search for him.

Marian appeared to noticed her distraction as she whispered, "Yes. He's still here floating around. You know. You have the look of a girl in love."

"Nonsense. Like all girls he has created a certain allure in me also."

"Yes. But you're the only one receiving a reflected . . . as you said—allure."

Was it that obvious? She needed to be careful not to send the wrong message. It could be deadly in her position. "I hope to work for Conseco for a long time and think building a good connection is essential."

"Whatever. But right now, a ride home from him would be a good connection for me."

Balarie bit her lip as she knew she would never win this point. "I'll see if I can find him." She shifted her position and searched for him.

After finding Tommy standing near the front of the boat, she watched him talking to Antonio who organized the dance, and a guy who Tommy appeared to admire. She would love to hear more about this relationship later.

She stepped forward to capture their attention. "Hello. So there you are."

Antonio turned to her. "We were talking about you . . . well I was trying to talk about you but Conseco doesn't want to tell me much about you. I think he wants to keep you under wraps until we face off in a competition later."

"What competition?"

"There's a major competition in the city in a couple of months. I've been trying to get him to enter for the last few years. This time I won't take no for an answer, and especially since he found a girl like you."

"I'll take that as a compliment, but I'm far from a professional."

"After two months of lessons you'll dance as beautifully as Tommy. You have a natural flow about you that many girls don't.

American girls are too timid to dance with a flair for the dance. However, being shy doesn't appear to be a problem for you. The connection tonight on the floor looked absolutely beautiful."

Tommy remained speechless, but his eyes revealed many unanswered questions. His intense stare made her wonder what it was he had on his mind. Did she do something wrong—or something right?

Antonio acknowledged the connection and cleared his throat. "It has been an incredible night and I want you to think about it, both of you. I think I need to find Marcie and call it a night."

Tommy acted as if he was recovering from a deep sleep. "Yes, it has been. Thank you for coming. I'll have the limo take you home. I think I would like to stay a while and have the driver come back later for me."

"It's nice out tonight." Antonio turned to Balarie and reached for her hand, and kissed the back of it in a slow show of chivalry. "I do hope to see you again, and hopefully on the dance floor."

Tommy turned to Balarie. "Please give me a minute to say good bye to everyone. I want you to stay with me if you can."

He sent a clear message—he wanted private time to talk to her. Now, maybe she could see what he had on his mind all night. "Sure. Tomorrow's Sunday so I can sleep late."

She shivered slightly in the late night breeze. As the perfect gentleman, he removed his coat and placed it around her shoulders. "I'll not be long."

###

Tommy found the rest of his guests and thanked them for coming. A feeling of accomplishment filled him as another great night had come to an end. He turned to Michael. "You did a great job. Tell the staff for me I'm happy."

"I understand you'll be staying a while tonight."

"Yes. I'm enjoying the nice weather, and I have some things to discuss with Balarie. Tell the driver for me that I'll call him when and if I need him."

"Are you planning on staying the night, sir?"

"I'm not sure, but make sure my state room is ready, if you will."

"Very good, sir. I'll check it for you. Let me know if you need anything else."

"I think that will be all." Tommy knew Michael wanted to turn in soon to his own room onboard. He was the only person who lived full time on the yacht. It actually cost him much less than hiring a guard to watch over it.

Michael paused for a second. "I almost forgot. The bartender mentioned you opened an expensive bottle of wine tonight. There are two glasses left in it, and it would be a shame to waste it."

"Thanks for reminding me. I'll stop by the bar and thank him." The thoughts of the delicious wine added the perfect closing to a great night.

He soon planned his words in advance as he climbed the stairs holding the two glasses of wine. Why was he nervous? What made her so special, and so far above other women he knew?

She remained in the same place he left her minutes ago. With her back to him, he watched her without being noticed himself. A gentle breeze carried her perfume, which was a delicate scent he couldn't name. While the top of his boat allowed a wide range of people to see them, they were far enough away not to be identified as anyone in particular.

With both hands full, he couldn't reach an arm around her like he wanted to. "Sorry, it took me so long."

She turned and faced him. "Not a problem. I've enjoyed the view and peaceful feeling here. I've never been on a long boat ride before. I was imagining how it could be great to see the world in such a boat."

Tommy handed her the wine glass. "The guy who handles my onboard cellar said this was peaking now. He's usually never wrong."

She accepted the wine. "I'll agree it's a robust wine. Does he work for you full time on the boat?"

"No, I only retain one full time guy who lives on it—the manager you met earlier." With one arm free he reached around her to offer a hug, nothing too intimate or overly friendly, just a comforting gesture in response to the cool breezes.

"How many long trips have you made with this boat?"

"None. It has only been out to sea a few times. I had intentions of making trips when I purchased it, but I've never taken the time. With a full crew, she has the range to travel around the world with adequate stops along the way. It would require a crew of six, which is what it has available. It also has six state rooms which could provide a passenger load of twelve."

"I notice it was a large boat from the top. I would like to see the rest of it some time."

"After we finish the wine I would love to show you. However, the manager's room we will not disturb. I know he had a busy day arranging all of this."

"He certainly did." As Balarie raised the glass to her lips, Tommy studied their fine line and soft impression on the glass as she sipped.

He moved closer to her as his hormones had to be rushing out of control for him to be thinking what he did. Still her lips glistened in front of him like bait in front of a hungry fish, and he could only resist it for so long.

After finishing the glass with no more words spoken, the silence added a blanket of comfort he hadn't known in a long time. He felt no need to pass unnecessary conversation. The silence spoke much louder than the words he had already forgotten to use. His arm pulled her closer which ignited his hunger for more.

"I think I owe you a tour." He used his arm to turn her more in his direction.

"It would be nice." Her eyes closed as he leaned closer, offering, he assumed, the right for him to advance. The glistening sparkle on her lips exceeded his ability to resist. Inches from them, primal instincts dominated his last hope of stopping a mistake. He couldn't do this—but he did.

The slightest of touches electrified his mind with a sweet surrender he would have to deal with later. He pressed forward with more authority as he felt her accepting his lips on hers. The warmth registered first and then next the softness, as the infusion of her lips melting into his continued.

He breathed in through his nose, not allowing his lips to part. Since she allowed this one, he didn't want to take a chance for

her to recover and deny the next. His hand found its way to the back of her head allowing him to increase the pressure on her lips. She kissed back. There was no mistake—she enjoyed it to.

After having received a pleasure he would treasure for a long time, he slowly pulled away from her, but added one last teasing kiss as he did. He needed to say something, but what?

She lowered her head against his shoulder. Life just got complicated. He glanced to his side and breathed easier. They were on his boat, and it was secure. No one would see them or suspect anything.

She quivered as he held her. He needed to go inside to keep her from getting any colder. The outfit she wore was scanty to say the least. Images of her dancing refilled his mind—powerful images of her standing toe to toe with him before rejecting him only to rejoin him time after time. No one had made him enter the character of the dance like this before.

Tommy turned sideways to allow her to walk beside him. He took slow steps to the stairways leading to the rest of the boat, knowing it would take a while to see it all, knowing he only had one room he really wanted to be in—his stateroom.

Minutes later, he stepped inside his private world on the boat. Outside the crew, no one else had ever seen it. It remained strictly off limits when he hosted parties, or had taken it out for the very few trips it had made. The day trips were nice, but required so much planning. He could only imagine the work involved in traveling for a long time on it. Still, he wanted to make such a trip one day.

The manager had been inside. Tommy saw a bottle of champagne waiting on him in a bucket of ice. Fresh flowers from the party, no doubt, had been redirected as well as some cheeses and fruits which had been prepared for his guest.

Tommy turned before shutting and locking the door behind him. He quickly glanced at her for any reaction to his intentions. The next few minutes could be critical as he motioned to the champagne. "It appears Michael is very perceptive."

"Either that, or used to you seducing

girls on your boat." She raised an eyebrow in a teasing, yet playful motion.

"The truth is simple. No one has seen this room outside the staff. This is a first for me. Now, don't go thinking I'm a mid-aged virgin. I'm far from it, but I'll admit I'm a workaholic extraordinaire."

"I'll admit I've heard many rumors about you."

"Really or should I ask?"

"Oh, where to start. With models around you day and night, most playboys would place you on a plateau as an idol."

"I think you know me already enough to know I never touch the models who work for me."

"I think so, but you have to admit it would be so tempting. And we both know they would gladly service you anytime and anywhere."

"I'll not argue the obvious, but offer this one defense. With all of the attention on my life, you'd think that at least one such proven scandal would have surfaced by now."

"True. But with your money, indiscretions can be silenced." She nodded her head in another show of seduction. "You'll have to answer one question for me."

"Such as?"

"Of all of the beautiful woman in the city, why me?"

"I think I can answer you best with a question—why not you?" He didn't wait for an answer as he closed the gap between them. Enough talking. His lips found the mark and entered into a heaven he had felt a few minutes ago on the top of the boat. This time he expected more which she must have anticipated as she opened her mouth as if to beg for his tongue.

As the moment turned into minutes he realized he hadn't kissed so passionately in a long time. It felt so natural for him to slip an arm under her and lift her. The bed wasn't far away, but still he wanted to carry her, and to place her where he wanted her to be, beside him and snuggled under the covers.

She shifted from his arms as he lowered her to the bed and rested on the edge. He moved in next to her and hugged her from the side as he leaned closer to her neck, and kissed the soft flesh of her nape. He heard a soft moan which excited him to go further. He removed his coat from her and tossed it to one side.

This revealed her body down to the top of her breasts which were barely covered by the dance outfit.

Her firm looking breasts had excited

him from the first time he saw her cleavage, and he could only imagine what her nipples looked like. He knew he wouldn't be disappointed. However, he wanted to move slowly and not scare her—not now with him so close.

He massaged her bare shoulder and expanded his reach to reach lower on her chest. She showed no resistance. He had reached a point of no return. The desire burned inside his body created a heated rush to his skin.

His right hand hunted for a zipper or a snap. How was it fastened? He could find nothing that worked. Frustrated, he shifted his emphases to her breasts and lowered his left hand to the top of the outfit and nudged it for a chance to slide inside. Although tight he managed to lift it enough to wiggle underneath. The nipple was much smaller than he imagined, but like a tiny jewel it quickly responded to his attention as he pressed it between his thumb and finger.

His other hand never could find the release. She responded to his frustration with a soft smooth whisper which confirmed his desire to know her thoughts on his actions. "Here. Let me help you. It's on the side."

"Ingenious." His mind analyzed the clever place to hide the seam, but for once he wanted to know something more than what a dress looked like on her. He wanted to know what it hid from him.

He found the zipper and worked it slowly. As it fell apart from her, the built in bra dropped with it. She shifted her weight to work it over the arm sleeve extending to her finger. Now naked from the waist up, he saw what he had dreamed of for many nights. As he lifted his black satin shirt over his head, he wanted to melt his skin next to hers. "Balarie, I love the way you work out."

Her hand massaged his chest as he curled his hand around a breast to explore its fullness and which felt exactly as he had assumed.

She leaned into his arms as he pressed his chest next to her skin. The skin on skin feeling excited him beyond his expectations. He reached for her dress again and pulled it lower as he worked a hand under the front and down toward her crotch. He reached lower and found her panties where he stopped for a second. This outfit was special. He didn't want to ruin it, but his passion wouldn't be delayed for long.

"Here let me help you lean back. I don't want to tear this outfit." He forced himself to be tender. Not that he wanted to hurt her, but his control was fading by the second.

As she obeyed his suggestion and leaned backwards, he managed to slide it down to her knees, and with her white panties rolled slightly lower, it presenting him with a new sexy view that teased him so slight with a peek of her crotch.

He stood beside her and handled her dance clothes with care as he placed it on the other side of the bed. As he finished, the sight of the panties hiding the last of her virtues pushed his resistance to the last point of no return. He reached for them and lowered them.

"Okay, what do you think?" She allowed him to see her straight on, with the lights on and without embarrassment. But he had seen many naked women. This woman he wanted to do more with than watch. He wanted to have sex. He wanted to penetrate her as soon as he could. Enough with foreplay or delays. He wanted her now.

"I think you're absolutely beautiful." He stood to unbuckle his pants as he noticed her watching him. Okay, his time to strip for her. He dropped his pants in record time and followed with his boxers.

"I hope you have protection."

Damn! He hadn't had sex in so long he had forgotten. Did he have a supply in a side drawer—he doubted it. Now what? It hit him—she wouldn't allow him inside her without one and he also knew better. He didn't want to father a baby, at least not right now.

"I'm not believing this." She used her elbows to lift her weight off her back.

"As I said, it has been a while since I had a girlfriend. I hope my confession doesn't disappoint you too much."

He watched her turn to her small clutch purse. "This is one emergency I might be able to handle, but no guarantees."

Watching with the interest of an addict anticipating a drug, he held his breath. She zipped open one side and peeked inside. Her face gave no indication of what she had discovered. The wait tormented him. A slow demur smile followed. "Call it a lucky day." She fished out a single condom. "I hope it fits."

He watched her study him. His erection had reached high alert. Whatever it took, he would stretch it over his tool. "Give me a second, and I'll make it work." It was easier said than done—he was a big guy.

Finally he snuggled next to her, feeling confident in the outcome. She kissed him immediately with a new sense of intimacy and opened her mouth to accept his tongue where she sucked on it relentlessly. His thoughts drifted to oral. Not now, but one day.

He used his hand to spread her legs. Her smooth shaved skin allowed him to explore her folds easily. He wanted to make sure she was ready for him. She was. Still, he wanted to bring her close to the edge of coming. Her increased breathing indicated he worked the right magical button on her clit.

As if he didn't know, she moaned. "That's it—that's the place."

He increased the rhythm and the pressure, as she uttered a small scream followed by a loud squeal of ecstasy. "I'm ready. I want you inside me. Please!"

Penetration is exactly what he wanted also. He didn't need to hear her repeat the request. He rolled on top of her. She spread her legs wider and curled them around his legs which pulled his manhood into position.

"Please let me know if it hurts." He inched closer to her as the anticipation drove him close to insanity.

He felt her grab his butt and thrust her hips at him. Ready—hell! Damn yes she was ready. He drove inside her, fully knowing what she wanted. He knew he stretched her as her nails dug into his back. He paused for a second and tried again, this

time she accepted all of him. Not just his throbbing dick, but all of his
being. He never did anything half ass. And this would be no exception.
He had found the one—that is, if she would agree with his plans for the future.

Chapter 17

The next morning Balarie woke wrapped in the arms of a man she had only know for a few days. Yes, she had heard of romances happening in a blink of an eye, but never believed it. She watched him breathing peacefully beside her before she glanced at the clock—she never slept to ten.

She quietly slipped from the bed and walked to the shower. Her hair looked worst than she could ever remember. The heavy hairspray had left her a mess. However, she had nothing to repair the damage. What could she do—wash it and let it air dry. Yuck.

The hot water felt good as it helped to wash memories of the night before away. She lathered twice to remove the sticky spray. What was she going to do after she washed? She only had the dance outfit with her.

After toweling dry, she wrapped it around her and walked out to the bedroom. As she passed by, Tommy opened his eyes.

"Wow! I see you're awake early."

"Yes. It's later than I thought."

Tommy held out his arms to her. "Come here."

Balarie edged over, and rested beside him, as he offered her a hug. "I don't have anything to wear home but the dance outfit. I didn't know I was coming here, or I would have taken something else with me."

"I see. We'll have to find you something."

"No, it's okay. I do need to get home and change. I have some work I need to do today to be ready for the meeting tomorrow."

"Yes, Dedication will get you everything." He leaned closer and kissed her bare shoulder as she became actually aware she had nothing under the towel.

She had made love to him last night, but today was another day. She still didn't know how it happened so fast, and what would become of it.

"Do you really need to go? We can spend some time here today if you want to." He rose on his elbows to stretch. "At the meeting tomorrow I need to talk to everyone about a trip to Milan. Several of the models I'm taking with me don't have passports. I also have one special person joining me on this trip."

The reality hit her. He was going to Milan with models days after he made love to her. And which special person? More importantly, a trip to Milan meant a plane ride. Nope, not going to happen. "I see. I'm sure it can be worked out for you." She wasn't ready to fly and might not ever be able to.

"I saw some photos of you a few days ago that Ethan had taken. You could still do well as a model. I see a great personality in your work, and something many girls can't pull off. Not only are you photogenic, but you bring such a high sense of raw sexy energy to the studio."

"What? Ethan showed you the photos he made of me?"

"Yes. I walked in a few minutes after you left the other day. He was just finishing up."

"So is that why you invited me into your bed last night? Did the photos really turn you on that much?"

He looked shocked, but she assumed he would when she confronted him.

"Listen, I really need to go."

"No, it's not like that."

"Okay, I believe you, but I still need to go. Can you call me a cab?" She lied. She felt confused and tired. She needed time to rest and think.

"I can have my driver take you home if leaving is what you really want."

She leaned over and kissed his cheek. "I did enjoy dancing with you."

"I'm sure this will not be the last time we'll dance. Are you sure you will not stay for a while?"

He rubbed her arm in a soothing compassionate way, but no, she needed time to think.

###

As Balarie walked into her apartment, she allowed the frustration to escape—what in the hell did she do last night? She slept with the boss, and the guy known to fire people for almost no reason at all. And then she walked out on him this morning. She used her hands to cover her face.

While he acted like he cared about her and the dancing felt extraordinary the night before, first thing this morning he announces he's going to Milan with several beautiful models. Yeah, like sure he's not going to bang them when he has a chance. She softly cried as she walked to her bed.

Still, the night before retained a certain magical quality she couldn't forget. For someone used to getting it all of the time, he acted unprepared for her. She did have to provide the condom. Was he telling the truth? Did he really never touch his models and have no girlfriend? How was she to really know?

She had work to do to get ready for the meeting tomorrow. Now, more than ever, she needed to be ready. She had great news to share. It would be so good to see him proud of her. She had to calm down.

She glanced at the blinking light on her phone. Someone had left a message. She could guess who. Since she did work for him, she eased toward it to listen to the message. Surprisingly, it was Joe checking on her instead. At least she could always count on him.

She retrieved the phone and returned his call. He would never believe this.

His voice sounded excited as he answered. "Hello, Balarie. Have you seen the papers today?"

"No. I just got home—why?"

"You don't have one photo in the times, you have three of them. And do you look like wow in your dress."

She knew there was a strong possibility of this happening. This could be good or bad. "I need to see it."

"You're not still with Tommy, are you? The paper said you left with him last night."

Yes, she really needed to read the article

now. "No, he's planning a trip to Milan."

"Are you going with him?"

"You know there's no way I'm getting on a plane."

"You need to get over this fear. Listen, I have a friend who lives next door and is a psychologist. I'll see if I can talk her into coming with me."

"I don't know about this."

"I insist. Get us some coffee on and I'll stop for some croissants for you and some bagels for me. I'll be by as soon as I can arrange it." The phone line died.

Balarie needed to confront her flying problem sometime, but not now. It would take much more than a onetime meeting to help her. She stood and glanced at a mirror. The outfit she loved earlier now looked bad on her. She hated it, and wanted to tear it to treads. It took pure will power not to do so.

Balarie had company coming, but since it was Sunday, she pulled out an old pair of jeans and a pull over t-shirt from her old university days at Georgia Tech. She closed her eyes for the moment and realized how much had changed since then when life was so simple.

She walked to the kitchen and started the coffee. A pad of paper caught her eye as she grabbed a pen and worked on her presentation for tomorrow. She needed to touch base with Samantha also to make sure she had the signed contract before the meeting. She couldn't afford any mistakes.

Two hours later Balarie heard a knock on her door. She walked over and allowed Joe and a girl with short, dark-black hair and matching glasses to walk in.

Joe motioned to his friend. "This is Sara."

Balarie turned to Sara. "Hi, I'm Balarie. Come on in and make yourself comfortable. I finished the first pot, but I'll make some more coffee if you will give me a minute."

Sara removed the glassed and shawl that she wore. "It sounds like you drink a lot of coffee."

"I've been known to. I know it's not good for me, but some habits are hard to break." Balarie could already feel the analysis beginning.

Joe walked to the table and placed a newspaper in the center. "I thought you might like to see this."

"Thanks, I guess. How bad is it?"

"The photos are really good, actually."

"And the write up?"

"That you'll have to decide for yourself." Joe pulled out a chair for Sara and stared at the coffee pot. "Here. You read and I'll make the coffee."

The headlines grabbed her attention—TOMMY CONSECO'S NEW GIRLFRIEND. "Oh shit!"

"Perhaps we need to add a wee bit of Irish spirits to the coffee." Joe's eyes widen.

"Top left drawer." Balarie read fast as her heart pounded. She had no clue how Tommy would react to this, but he had been in the spotlight forever. However, she also knew this was the one part of his life, his reputation, which he defended with a vengeance.

Balarie flipped to where the story continued. Then she saw the two next photos, one of her dancing with Tommy and one with her leaving with him as she stepped inside his limo. Her eyes refocused on them dancing. The strong intense emotions displayed in the dance could be interrupted differently by many people, and especially by those not accustomed to the style.

Joe walked back over to his seat. "Damn, I wish I could have been there."

Thoughts of the night returned. "Yes, the dancing was fun and I survived. I was, like, really nervous. By the way, I need to contact Lenny, the designer. I'm sure he's more than happy about getting such publicity out of this."

"Oh . . . I'm sure he is." Joe pointed to another section in the article. "They even mentioned his name here."

Balarie half closed her eyes to think. "I don't remember mentioning the designers name last night. I wonder how the reporter knew this." She suddenly realized, however, it could have been planted by someone inside the agency, perhaps Ethan himself.

Sara smiled for the first real time since she walked in. "You appear to be taking this okay. I'm still a little lost on what's going on."

Balarie wondered how much Joe had told her. "I was invited to a tango dance last night and I think it got a little out of hand. Or, at least, the papers make it appear that way."

"So, I take it Tommy isn't your boyfriend."

Balarie paused before she answered. The fast pace of the last week gave her little time to think about what was going on. Last night was definitely a shocker. "I've only been working at the

agency for a little over a week and met Tommy when I interviewed with the agency."

"I see. But sometimes life changes on a dime, as they say." She made a jester of sniffing the air. "The coffee does smell good."

Joe stood to retrieve a cup for everyone.

"Yes, but not always smooth. However, since he told me he was going to Milan in a few days, I'll have some time to think."

Sara turned to Joe. "I think this is why Joe wanted me to come by here with him. He tells me that you have a fear of flying."

"A fear would put it mildly."

"Have you worked with anyone to get over this?" Sara accepted the cup from Joe before returning her attention to Balarie.

"I have some, but nothing works. I haven't worked on it too hard. I think it's easier for me to simply avoid the situation of having to fly."

"But then you miss out on trips like the one to Milan, am I right?"

"Okay, for starters, he hasn't actually invited me yet."

"Why do I get the indication you managed to nip his invitation in the bud."

Balarie wondered how Sara managed to find the right cliché comment at the appropriate time. She quickly reflected on the meeting this morning. She had ended it quickly and left. Down deep, she hoped he wouldn't and didn't know how to handle it if he did. Would this cost her a job she had dreamed of for years?

Joe acted more sympatric. "I did read recently the number of people scared of flying is much higher than generally assumed. Surely there's some ways it can be handled. Perhaps she can take a drug of some kind."

"Sedation can help to some extent, but the best way to get over any fear is to face it." Sara tasted the coffee. "Humm, not bad."

"I've never been on a plane, and don't plan to any time soon."

"I understand, but I do have a question for you."

"Yes."

"Are you prepared to live with other fears caused by your not flying?"

Without knowing the exact details of her past, Sara had hit a nerve with icy cold precision. She remembered the day she quit working for a modeling agency and wanted to find a different way to make a living. The assignment, a week-long jump to the Caribbean's to highlight a travel article would have been snapped up by most models, but on location would mean flying. When pressed, she had no option but to tell the truth. At first they understood, but she knew she had burned a bridge to the agency and the sponsor.

Sara patiently waited for an answer.

Balarie knew the technique—when you ask a question—you wait on the answer. Still, the pressure mounted for her to respond. "It has cost me before and I'm sure it will again."

"Let me try a straightforward approach. What is it about flying you find scary?"

"The crash. I'm sure everyone has a fear of dying, am I right?"

"Yes, it's a primal fear which has also kept many people alive to see a happy long life. What makes you think the plane might crash? I'm sure you have seen how much safer it is than say driving a car."

"I don't know. Maybe it's the loss of control and with my life in their hands. Also remember, the plane is mechanical, and mechanical things break."

"Both of these are common reasons." She lifted the coffee cup to her nose again and sniffed. "Have you ever had something mechanical fail on you and hurt you before?"

At first she couldn't think of anything. Then her dreams reentered her mind. "I have times I'm in a ride at an amusement park and my ride is flying loose."

"I see. Has this ever happened to you?"

Memories of when she was eight replayed in her mind as if it was happening to her again. She reached for the arms on her chair. "Yes, once when I was a child. A chain snapped on a chair swing, you know like the kind they awing far from the center post, and about twenty feet off the ground."

"Were you hurt?"

"No, the operator managed to slow the ride immediately, but I knew it was all over for me. Others weren't so lucky and had to go to the hospital. I still remember the ambulances taking them away." Balarie used her hands to cover her face.

"I understand how you must have felt. The good news is that I think I can help you, but it will depend upon how much you want to help yourself." Sara turned to Joe. "This coffee is good, can I have another?"

###

Balarie poured another late afternoon coffee as she wondered how to get something quick to eat. The day had disappeared fast as she prepared to work late into the night. Marian and Linda from the night before promised to be by her office soon.

Her phone rang. It was Samantha.

"Hi. I hopped you would call me back. I had a brain storm last night and thought you might like to see what I was thinking." Balarie held her breath as she waited on an answer.

"I'm listening. And by the way, you

wore one hell of a dress last night. I thought you and Conseco didn't know each other until last week."

"Thanks, the dress was by Andrew and designed for me during a fast two day period. You know how Conseco loves to dance. The papers as you can imagine blew it all out of proportion. We danced at a party and he invited many people back to his boat for an after party."

"Well, you could've fooled me, which is hard to do these days. I thought I was the one starting this budding romance. Now tell me about your idea."

"I know you want to highlight how to dress your boyfriend, but have you thought on who will be in the background and introducing the guys?"

"Not really, and I assumed we didn't need anyone."

"Okay, but let me ask you this. When you see, for example, Mr. Conseco out on the town, *what* or should I say *who* is always around him?"

"He has a reputation of being around beautiful women. After all, he does own one of the top modeling agencies in the city."

"Precisely, and which is why I think the hottest guys should also have their following. I think I know the perfect models to do the job, and ones with a following of their own."

"Interesting. I can only guess."

"I wanted to ask your opinion on this before I present it at the meeting tomorrow morning."

"Good. I'll have a signed contract to you by eight thirty tomorrow. I can add a note on there if you wish. I actually kind of like it, as I'm digesting what you're suggesting."

"Thank you. The two models I have in mind are on their way here also. I'll send you more information on what we all brainstorm in a few hours."

"I'll be here working late so let me know when you're done and we can order a drink somewhere."

"Absolutely."

Shortly afterwards, Marian and Linda walked in all eager and full of questions, as they must have stayed up all night analyzing the situation. Their youthful appearance without heavy makeup made them appear much more like trusted friends than fake beauty queens from the night before.

"Hello. I hope you're doing better than me today. I need more coffee. How about you?" Balarie wanted to continue the low key meeting and ask for their help. She felt so close to nailing this and wanted to make sure what she proposed made sense.

"Coffee sounds good." Marian turned toward the hallway. "I know where it is and I'll be back in a minute."

Good. Balarie would have time alone with Linda. As she studied Linda, she remembered her own career in modeling, and how the world seemed at her finger tips and only higher mountaintops lay in front of her. Then, she remembered the day her world changed. They wanted her to go on location to shoot. She still couldn't believe she had said no to the largest account they had?

Balarie's stomach tightened with the memories. Knowing she would be fired, she quit. Her manager learned the secret and kept it. Good for her, but bad for Balarie. There was no way she was going to fly to the Caribbean islands on a plane— any plane.

It wasn't a time to lapse into self-pity. She pulled her thoughts back to the present. "I think I mentioned what I had in mind last night."

"Yes, and we've been talking about it. We love the idea!" Of course she did, if it meant work.

"It would be easy to use girls at random for the backgrounds and attraction but I think it would be more memorable if we used the same two girls and gave them a mysterious on the edge reality and one which would mesmerize the girls who will be reading the ads into a sense of wanting to be these girls. Is this making sense to you?" Balarie asked.

"Yes. Definitely. Girls always want to know what other girls think before they jump in. They also want to think they do it before others."

"Good. Then here is what we need to work on today. I don't know of anyone who has more experience in being in the background than you two. This is a time for you to express what you really want to accomplish in such a role. I also think we can capitalize on the past photos of you with Conseco. This plan I still have to sell to him and it is what I'll be presenting in the meeting tomorrow."

"I'll have to say you have guts. Just remember, this is your idea and not mine, that is, unless you're successful."

"I understand where you're coming from, and I'll not ruin your chances to work with Conseco. I promise."

Marian looked very relieved as Linda returned. "I think our ship just came in."

Chapter 18

As Tommy placed his perfectly smelling morning coffee on the corner of his desk, he shifted through the company reports and billings covering the last week's activity. He paused at Balarie's near zero production. While she had only been with them for a week, she had lined up some work. He realized the pressure she would feel at the meeting in a few hours. She never returned his call last night.

While he thought everything had been great on Saturday night, he wondered why she wanted to leave so quickly on Sunday morning. If it was to prepare for this meeting, she shared his same drive and determination—both a good and a bad thing.

After Saturday night he wanted to experience the same high again on Sunday. He wished she had at least returned his call. They needed to talk, to sort things out. The one time he had broken his rules of no sex had sent mixed visions which haunted him and robbed any chance he had of sleeping.

Tommy made another trip to get coffee. It wasn't so much that he wanted such, but more in a hope that he would casually bump into Balarie. He made the circle around the executive floor. Her door remained closed. While he could knock on it, he hesitated.

As he started around the loop again, he noticed Joe in his seat and retracted his steps. It wouldn't be long until the meeting. One more cup of coffee and he would be bouncing off the wall.

With his mind lost in his thoughts of having sex again with Balarie, his head jerked sideways at the sound of his assistant knocking on his door. "Sir, the meeting is about to start."

Showtime. He wanted to know where the company stood on many projects, and see how much word had gotten out on his Saturday night fling. He also wanted to hear what Balarie had planned for him. He straightened his suit and adjusted his laces on his Cuban heeled shoes.

Without saying a word, he marched to the meeting room next to his. All seats were filled as he surveyed the group. Balarie had taken a seat closer to his right. "Good morning everyone. I hope you all had a great weekend." He glanced at Balarie and decided to hit any rumors about them head on. Well kind of, as he paused briefly.

"I assume everyone saw the photos in the paper of Balarie and me dancing." He heard the various comments coming all at once. He raised his hands to silence the group. "I think we received some good press and we need to capitalize on it."

"Exactly!" Balarie's voice interrupted him with a sudden flare. It would be good for everyone to hear from her and it might take him off the hook in explaining the situation as she continued, "I know I have everyone's attention, but I hope it will be worth it later when I give my report. And yes, I loved to dance with Mr. Conseco."

Tommy loved the simple way Balarie handled the situation—not saying too much or too little. He could only imagine what she had in her report. "It's good to see someone taking the initiative. And for the record, I was highly surprised to learn I had hired such a skilled dancer." He glanced around the room and couldn't decide if he had nullified the floating rumors or started new ones.

He claimed his seat at the end of the conference table and opened his file. The charm and wit mixed with a clean all American look placed Balarie above all girls he had ever met. The images of making love to her pressed all other thoughts from his head, and made concentrating on the meeting almost impossible. He had to talk to her as soon as it ended.

After floating through the meeting, he waited for Balarie's time to present. His attention focused on her mesmerizing walk to the front of the table directly across from him.

"I know I have only been here a week, and what a week it has been. I feel so fortunate in connecting with one of our buyers. I think everyone knows Samantha Kuppel. A few minutes before the meeting she faxed over a signed invoice for a project we have worked on. She had the main idea but loved a twist we added over the weekend."

A round of applause followed. Did she really manage to pull off a major sale so quickly? Hell yes, he felt impressed.

"The major theme in this monthly article will be on . . . how to dress your boyfriend for success. The emphases will be on normal, well almost normal guys, who still have a masculine college preppy look. While the rest of the world highlights muscle

builders and the supermodel look, our mission is how to make the normal good looking guy look successful."

One manager spoke eagerly. "Have you selected the models for this yet?"

"I have the first three selected, but they haven't been notified yet. The rest will be added as we come closer to the production date. This will also give us some time to analyze and perfect our approach."

Tommy clapped his hands in a solo display of appreciation. "And you said you added a twist. Can you explain what you mean?"

"This was added last night and is still being fine tuned. It's also a reason I didn't want to make a full announcement until I received some input from everyone here." Tommy watched her slow deliberate turn to face him. "The interesting part or twist came from inspiration I received from you."

Flattery only extended so far. Would she disclose their night together? Surely not!

"You've built a reputation of having beautiful women around you. It has worked great in building your image. If we invade upon your magic for these average guys that we want to promote, I think it will do magic for them as well."

"Having beautiful women around a guy promoting a product is nothing new."

"Yes, many times the women are often

forgotten, but what if over time you used the same girls building a mystic following of them. What do you think would be the chance of also landing them a major endorsement?"

Another booker glanced at her sideways. "Extremely high. Do you have anyone in mind?"

"Actually I do. I worked with two professional on this last night. I know this will be up to you, but I talked to Linda and Marian, the two models from the dance last Saturday night, and picked their brains on how they perfected their way of shadowing you."

"Really. You know I use different girls all of the time to kind of spread the exposure around."

"Yes, but you always seem to have them portray the same look. What I was after is the mindset of a girl on the side and how to best present this image."

Tommy thought about her comments. She had nailed it. It also allowed him a way out of the media cross hairs knowing this would be an easy sale. But what would this do their relationship? He smiled at her as he studied a professional high driving woman in front of him. Did their night together mean anything to her?

The rest of the meeting went smoothly.

As Tommy ended the session, he motioned for Balarie to join him. "I like your idea . . . really. Can you stay for a few minutes? There's something else I want to mention to you."

"Sure. I thought you might have some questions."

As the last person left, he moved closer to Balarie. "I tried to call you last night."

"Sorry. I went home late and worked on this to nearly midnight."

"I see. About the other night."

She interrupted him, "I don't know what to say. That's so unlike me."

"And me too. I honestly am not the playboy that many people think I am. You're the first girlfriend for me in a long time." Girlfriend? He didn't intend to use that particular word, but what word could he use to describe her?

"I can see we need to talk."

"Yes. And I know the perfect place to discuss this. I tried to tell you about a trip to Milan we need to make in about two weeks." Tommy tried to read her facial expressions—was it panic or something worst?

She backed from him. "I can't go to Milan."

"Why not?"

"Sorry, I just can't."

Rejection hit hard. The frustration mounted, but he forced himself to remain in control. "I thought we had a beautiful night together. For what it's worth, it was the best ever for me. I was hoping it was the same for you." He turned and walked out of the door before he said too much more.

Chapter 19

Balarie needed time to think. She had no idea she would be asked to fly so soon. She rushed into her office and closed the door only to hear Joe knocking on it seconds later. He opened it without permission. What was she going to do? He was perhaps her best friend and much more than her assistant.

"I take it your ideas didn't fly."

"No, they liked it. Tommy wants me to go to Milan with him."

"Yes, you mention he had a trip planned."

"Now, he wants me to go with him, and the trip is only in a couple of weeks. I think he also wanted to talk about last Saturday night."

"Okay, so what are you going to do?"

"I told him that I couldn't go. I didn't give him a reason. I couldn't. I have no idea what he's thinking now." She felt her knees shaking.

"Well, I enjoyed working here for a while anyway."

"You don't really think he'll fire me, do you?" Her heart pounded. She needed this job. She also wanted—no, she needed—to see what would happen to their relationship. Given time, it might work.

"Honestly, not after you brought in a major account, but you need to let him know you're scared of flying. Being honest is, as they say, always the best policy."

Balarie squeezed every muscle she had and fought the anguish inside for as long as she could. The slow release helped her to cope and think. "I hope you're right. I need to concentrate on this major sale. I'll need the right moment to tell him about my fear of flying." After seeing him almost every day the week before, she wondered how many times their paths would cross this one.

###

Tommy walked into his office and closed his door. She turned him down. This wasn't an invitation. This was business. Okay, maybe not all business since he wanted to find out more about her. Who exactly was she? If she planned on using the hard to get angle, she worked it to perfection.

The fact she landed a large sale added icing on the cake, but he had no reason to suspect she wouldn't be good in sales. She had the personality for it—that's why he hired her. This unexpected refusal had blindsided him. He flipped on his computer and searched the data files. The familiar photos he had studied for hours materialized on his screen.

One by one he restudied them. Why did she have such an effect on him? Another question: why did she quit modeling herself? It was time to find some answers. He didn't often check with owners of other agencies, but made exceptions from time to time. This was definitely one of them.

###

Balarie finished her day working on the case and hurried home. She had made several trips to the modeling school, looking for more guys she could use. Each time she left her office, she prayed she wouldn't run into Tommy. She needed the night to think. A bottle of wine and some take-out Chinese food would be all she needed to relax and do nothing.

The short nap from the night before left her with a headache and a druggy, drawn out feeling all day. With all she had on her mind concerning the modeling account, she effectively blocked out her personal relationship with Tommy. With the first glass of wine soothing her mood, she allowed her mind to drift back to his boat.

Did he plan to seduce her on it all along?
She shook her head. She didn't really think
so. If he did he would have at least have a
condom available.

She sipped on a long slow drink of the
wine, allowing it to filter down her throat.
It tasted nice, but nothing like the wine he
provided on the boat. The life he could
offer her was unbelievable. So why was she
fighting it so much?

She had no answers, and only more
questions. Her mind had been so focused
on doing well with this agency. Getting the
attention of Conseco, hummm . . . Tommy,
had to be part of her plan, but it was his
business attention she went after. Yet, she
giggled, he would definitely be an out of
this world catch for any girl. He had the
skills to make a great lover, but making
love was something which was to happen
later in a relationship, not days after you
meet.

She enjoyed another large sip of the
wine and shifted her thoughts to the trip to
Milan. She needed to understand more of
what this trip involved. She had frozen
when she heard him mention it. Why was it
so important?

Her head felt heavy with the wine and
lack of sleep. The main problem hidden
under everything involved her fear of

flying. A clear vision of the day of the accident flashed in front of her. What if she had died in that moment? Or, nearly as bad, been crippled for life?

She would call Joe's psychologist friend soon for help. Only miracles could help her now. However, many people flew. She needed to face it one day.

The next glass of wine empted the bottle. What was Tommy doing tonight? Cuddling with him would be nice. Making love to him again even better. To her the raw sexual image presented the best thought she could sleep on as she stumbled to her bedroom.

Chapter 20

Tommy walked into a small side restaurant in the Hilton. Earlier, when Tommy made the arrangements to lunch with Roberta Connelli, the owner of the agency where Balarie had worked earlier, he had breathed easier when she hadn't asked many questions. It was supposed to be a light conversation about the industry and the changes coming their way.

"Hello, Tommy. It's good to see you." She leaned over and offered him two cheek kisses, typical of her European background.

"It's likewise good to see you. We need to get together more often." Tommy waved at a waiter. "What can I order you to drink?"

"I don't drink much during the day. I still have a full schedule today, but I guess a glass of wine would be nice." She shifted in her chair.

"I know you're busy, like all of us. Are you planning on going to fashion week in Milan?"

"I don't really see how I can get out of

it. I assume you'll be going also."

"Yes, I'm making plans now. I had hoped one of my newest hires would be going, but she doesn't seem to want to. I think she worked for you earlier."

She laughed. "I know who you're talking about—Balarie."

"Yes. She's doing a great job otherwise and I'm glad she came looking for us. I know she worked for you, but I promise I didn't go after her."

"You can relax. I know more than you think. She left on her own. I learned after she left why. She's a very special girl and yes, I've seen you with her in the papers." She leaned over and winked. "I'm going to tell you something which will lock you in my debt forever."

"If it's insight into who she is, I'm sure I will be."

"I assume everything we say will be held in confidence." Her eyes sparkled with a sense of overflowing joy.

"Naturally. You can trust me, and I hope you can me as well."

"I offered Balarie a chance to make it big time with one of our top buyers. She turned it down. I went ballistic, as you know I

can from time to time." She studied her nails and acted like she needed no response. "Would you like to know why?"

"I think this is why I asked you to join me for lunch."

"Balarie is terrified of flying. She will not fly, and tried to keep this a secret from me. I lost her before I discovered the truth. I wish she had let me know instead of quitting. We had arranged a major assignment for Balarie, but she walked away from it when she learned she had to fly to the location."

"Damn! What a shame. In this business it's a necessity. However, it's something which can be overcome. I think."

"I've heard counseling can help, but more importantly she needs someone to support her as she overcomes those fears. She never gave us the chance."

"As you said, I think I'll be in your debt for a very long time." Tommy reached for his glass of wine wondering how to handle this problem. If he had a chance with her, he had to find a way to help her. He needed advice on how to proceed.

Chapter 21

Balarie felt much better after a full night sleep. She skipped the coffee when she reached her office and went immediately into making phone calls. While one major account helped, she still needed to maintain the ones the agency assigned her. The last one had thrown her a curve.

She walked to the management area and hoped for a miracle. "I need some help on this one. I received a request for a model to be nursing a baby for a baby formula company. Any suggestions?"

"I think we have several models who want to make some extra money. What's the problem?"

"The mother image will not be a problem. I'm thinking of the baby model."

"Oh, I see. I'll work on finding you one. It shouldn't be too hard. When do you need it?"

"In about three hours."

"Got ya. I'll find you one. Where will you shoot?"

"Here. It's an emergency situation. They

have copy, but forgot the *photo*." Balarie walked out, hoping they wouldn't let her down. The session had been scheduled already.

Three hours later, she walked down to the studio and saw Ethan in action. A beautiful, young girl was enjoying the painful new adventures of motherhood. Balarie didn't recognize her, but assumed she must be the real mother. "How is it going?"

Ethan glanced at Balarie for a split second. "This isn't my most cooperative model I've ever worked with. Excuse me."

Balarie walked to the side and allowed Ethan to work his magic. The baby moved often and made faces—not the ones the advertiser wanted—but faces. Balarie noticed a deep sensation in her breast as she watched. The thoughts of breast feeding an infant hadn't crossed her mind often, but she thought she could be a good mother.

A few minute stop turned into an hour. With too much time to think, she reflected on her life. At one time she wanted the American dream with a loving husband and kids. What happened? A career is what happened, and she knew it. A career she held by

threads now. They would also soon

know her fears. She would have to decide what would be her next move.

If she lost her job this time, she would move back to Atlanta and where she started. A life as a suburban wife wouldn't be too bad. In fact, the more she watched the baby, the more she wondered how she would be as a mother. Of course, a good husband might be a good place to start.

As the shooting ended, she was all ready for motherhood and the whole white picket fence thing. It wasn't a major account, but added some to her resume.

Ethan soon joined her as she finished the paperwork documenting the shoot. "It's good to see you here taking an interest in this assignment."

"I wanted to make sure it went off smoothly."

"I have more photos you might want to see from the dance the other night."

"Yes, I wanted to talk to you also about sending Conseco photos from my photo shoot. I didn't think those would be part of the agency files."

"Everything I shoot belongs to them. You should know that."

"I thought you were doing me a favor. I should've known."

"I've been working here for a long time. Listen, I know Conseco has taken a large interest in you. I've never seen him like this before. And to tell the truth, I'm good at spotting much more than what is on the surface. It has been my job to bring out the personality behind the models. So . . . it's hard to hide emotions from me." He winked and walked toward the set.

She wondered how many people knew they had an affair, and exactly how much they really knew. If the truth came out, what would Tommy do? She had heard about his image, and his reputation for a long time—everyone in the city had.

The more she worried about it, the more she also realized she enjoyed that night, and the intense feelings it released inside of her. Could it be real? Did he actually have feelings for her?

###

Tommy walked aboard his boat. Michael joined him with a firm handshake. "Are you sure you want to do this?"

"Absolutely, and we have a small time to get it all ready. I'll leave it to you to hire a crew and get her prepared. Do you see any problems?"

"No, sir. This will be magnificent. All will be in order."

"Good."

###

Balarie rushed back to her office, where

she saw Joe talking to an older woman sitting in a chair facing his desk. He turned and flashed a large smile. "You have a special guest who wants to meet you."

Not knowing the woman, Balarie walked closer to her. The charming looking lady in her sixties studied her without offering a smile. "Hi, I'm Mrs. Conseco. I would like to talk to you for a minute if I can."

The last name caught her attention. Was she related to Tommy?

"Sure. I just finished a shooting, but come on in." Balarie lead the way as Joe gave her a quick thumbs up sign. What was going on?

"I enjoyed seeing pictures of you with my son in the paper. I wanted to come see you in person. I hope you don't mind."

Okay, this is Tommy's mother. Balarie moved fast to direct Mrs. Conseco to a seat and waited for her before she moved to her own. "This is a surprise. What do I owe this pleasure to?"

"I'm sure Tommy doesn't talk about me much. He has a thing about privacy and all, but he's still my son. For the first time in a long time he wants me to go on a trip with him in a few weeks."

The Milan trip was in a few weeks. Was this the one she was referring to? "That's good to hear. I'm sure you'll have a good time in Italy."

"I hope so. He mentioned he wanted to take you with him, but you said you couldn't go. That's disappointing to me. I had high hopes of him finding a girl to settle down with this time."

"I've only known Tommy for a short time."

"I also know he allows very, almost no one, to call him Tommy, but people close to him, or those he wants to be close with."

Ooops, she should have said Mr. Conseco, but it slipped in talking to his mother. "We've spent some time together, but it has only been a little over a week since I met him."

"Sounds like his father and me. We married on the third day after we met."

A shock wave hit her. "Really?"

"Yes, and I never regretted it. But . . . I'm simply a mother running her mouth too much. I really wanted to just stop by and meet you while I was in the office. I actually came to see Tommy, but they say he's out at his boat now."

"I see. Perhaps he'll be back shortly."

"I can't wait for him. It's going to be so much fun going to see Milan. Tommy calls me his special lady now, but I think that honor will soon shift to you."

"I doubt it. He appears to be the kind of guy who will always treat his mother special."

Mrs. Conseco stood and tossed her head to one side. "Let's have lunch one day."

"Sure." As Mrs. Conseco left, Balarie understood who the special woman Tommy planned to take to Milan was. She felt a strange embarrassment flowing over her. Was he planning on introducing his mother to her? That would be fast—real fast.

Now the real question concerning their relationship entered her thoughts. She had misjudged him, and had cut him off before he could explain. She wanted to talk to him. She checked her watch. She needed to quit for the day soon anyway.

She walked out and nodded at Joe. "Thanks for warning me."

"I had no time on this one. I would have loved to be inside to hear what happened. You will tell me, right?"

"Maybe when I have a lot to drink." She watched him grin, and knew he would do that one night. "I need to check with Conseco's assistant and see how long he plans to be at his boat."

"I'm not even going to ask."

I know you will. She smiled briefly before she disappeared along the hallway. Soon, she stopped in front of Tommy's assistant. "I was leaving when I ran into Mrs. Conseco. She said her son is at his boat. Do you know how long he'll be there? I need to talk to him."

"I think for a while, but why don't you call him."

"Yes, I guess so." Balarie walked off, but knew that what she had to do, she had to do in person.

Chapter 22

Tommy rushed from one part of the yacht to the next as he handled one detail after another. In order to make fashion week in time he needed to leave in a week. The publicity would be extraordinary as he raced his boat across the Atlantic to attend the show. His selected guest for this trip would have little time to get ready.

He would leave the hiring of the crew in Michael's hands, which was why he paid him. The one person which would require his approval would be the captain. While he knew once out to sea the captain would be in full charge, he also had other plans for the captain while on the cruise.

He smiled at one additional special arrangement he would make. Maria, his housekeeper would be invited to go with them as one of the crew members. This way she could visit her family.

In the midst of his rush to get all ready, he heard a voice behind him. "Hello, Tommy. I heard I could find you here."

Tommy knew the voice, but never

expected Balarie to come unannounced. His preparation was to be a surprise. He turned slowly. "I'm not going to ask who told you I was here."

"I saw your mother a few hours ago."

"Mother?"

"Yes, she came by to check me out." Balarie walked closer to him. "The boat looks much different during the day."

"I agree, and she can be a handful at times."

"I think I left you kind of quickly the last time I was here. I need to tell you something, and I hope you understand why I became spooked."

Tommy failed to hide a grin he knew she would see. "I think I know now. You should've told me you have a fear of flying."

He watched her mouth open. "Someone told."

"I know I must have a badass reputation for someone special to me to not trust me and tell me things. We're going to have to work on that."

"I knew you might expect me to fly for business, and I really didn't want to hide this fact, but I . . . I really wanted to work for you."

"I know. I've run this company for a long time. It has grown tremendously since

I started it, consuming all of my life, and I know I'm not getting any younger. I guess what I'm saying is . . . I want to dance with one and only one girl for the rest of it."

Finally, she smiled. "But why me?"

"I'll answer with a question, why not?"

"I see we need to do some serious talking."

"Agreed. That's why I'm getting this yacht ready for the trip."

"What trip?"

"Since you surprised me here, I think it's time for me to surprise you. I really want you to go to fashion week in Milan. This way you'll not have to fly. Still, mind you, I plan to help you every step of the way of getting over flying, but later."

She looked shocked. "You would do this for me?"

"You said that we need time to talk. How does a week at sea sound?" He waited for an answer.

"There isn't a girl in the world who wouldn't like something presented to her like this. Can I trust you?"

"You can trust me to do only one thing. I'll try to seduce you into marrying me somewhere between here and Italy. I'll have my only living relative, my mother that you met, and a captain standing by. "

"When do I have to give you an

answer?"

"I know this is fast, but the boat has to leave in six days." He had hoped for a yes on the spot, but then again, he hadn't planned on seeing her today. He had wanted to set the mood for a date a day or two from now. At least she didn't say no. He studied her face, and assumed it was only a matter of time.

"Not much time for a girl to decide her future."

"I understand, but plenty of time to face her future and openly, truthfully talk about it. We'll have a week on board."

"Who will be onboard with us?"

"I'm working the list now, but I think we can discuss it if you wish. I think you know now that my mother will join us."

"Yes, and I like her by the way."

"The other guest I'm considering includes Joe, your assistant, and Olivia, my assistant, whom by the way, I think might like each other."

"No way. Joe likes men, strong virile ones."

"If you haven't noticed, Olivia is much more "manly" than most men. And I don't think she'll mind me saying this."

Balarie laughed. "I'll keep your comment a secret. Who else?"

"Antonio and Marcie, the couple who

organized the tango dance the other night want to go, and free tango lessons for several nights sounds like fun to me."

"Yes, it does sound intriguing."

"Since we need to get some work done, I also hope Samantha will join us. To round out the group, I want Ethan to be on board. He needs experience shooting runways, and this will be good for him to work Milan for the week. Additionally, he'll be needed to shoot layouts of Marian and Linda, the models you plan to use in your magazine articles on . . . humm, how to dress your boyfriend for success."

"Sounds like a full house."

"We also have a crew of six people. But remember one thing; this boat does have my private quarters totally separated from the main ship. It will be like we are completely alone for as long as you wish."

"Do you always move this fast?"

"I think the reason I'm successful is because I fill a need before my competition knows there's even a need. This . . . being ahead of the curve has served me well. I would hate to stand to the side while another guy moves in on you. So most definitely, I do move fast. Is that a problem?"

Balarie's expression turned serious. "I know we had a beautiful time the other night. And the sex was unbelievable and all. But you hardly know me. A seductive transatlantic cruise would turn any girls head. What I'm worried about is what happens after it's over. I don't want to be known as a one night or a one week girl. Does that make sense?"

Tommy nodded. "I understand, and this will give us some time to get to know each other better. With all of the hectic life in the city, I can think of no better way, can you?"

"If this doesn't work out, where will this trip leave me and my career?" She squirmed. "I'm a single woman in a city that plays hardball and you know it."

"All I'm asking for is a chance to get to know you better."

"Fair enough. I'll think about it, and let you know soon. I promise."

Tommy moved closer and invaded her resistance. "Listen. I know the future is scary. It is for all of us. I really want you to go with me to Milan." He leaned forward and kissed her lips softly, hoping to instill a sense of the fillings he had for her. It was nothing passionate, but only a simple connection, and a sense of caring he wished to share.

She kissed back and then leaned her head on his shoulder. Hopefully, time would finish his mission. He knew to be patient.

Chapter 23

Balarie slouched in the chair behind her desk. For two days she had hid in her office dodging the question. Was she going, or staying? She knew she needed to give Tommy an answer, and possibly today.

Last night she lay awake late into the night thinking of the great sex she had with him, and how it would be so damn incredible to know she could experience this night after night on the cruise. The urge to repeat that night with Tommy kept her awake all night.

She went to her computer and researched Tommy's life scattered all over the internet. She knew he was world famous and rich, but the full extent of his past, she could only guess. She also told herself she didn't want his money to distract her from what she really wanted in life—a husband who adored her and would be there for her when she turned old and gray.

She basically wanted to know why her? What was it she could bring to the table besides an appetite? He had his choice of endless beauties, which also brought up the trustworthy question. Perhaps he was right and the week at sea would give them a lot of time to talk. It could also be a major heartbreak in the works.

Balarie heard a commotion outside her door and Joe raising his voice to match someone else yelling loudly. What in the hell was going on?

She rushed to her door and opened it to find a tall muscular guy standing in front of her. His roughed jaw and fierce looking eyes descended on her as Joe reached for the phone. "You must be Balarie, the new booker."

While she saw no sense in lying, Balarie hesitated. She wanted to know what this mad man wanted.

"I thought you would at least recognize me from the photos, and if I remember, you still represent me."

Ahhh, he had to be one of the male models. She focused on his face looking for a match in her mind. Many of the bulky macho guys looked the same to her, but something registered. She needed a minute.

"Let me help you out, I'm Bobby Norton, the guy canned last week doing a photo shoot. You replaced me with some skinny runt."

Now, it came to her. "I didn't . . . can you, the buyer did. The photo he had of you and the way you looked on the set didn't match. You gained a lot of weight and muscles which isn't the look they wanted. The designer had a hard time fitting you in the outfits."

"I thought your job was to fight for us— not kill our assignments."

"I work hard every day finding you work. If you change your look you need to keep your photos current."

"Conseco's the one who wanted me to bulk up. I tried to see him, but he's not here."

Balarie had to control this. She glanced around and watched the crowds forming along the hallway. But did she really want to take this mad man behind closed doors? "I'm sure Tommy had some other work lined up for you. You did still get paid, didn't you?"

"I got a cancellation fee is all. Mostly, I lost a chance to land on a slick cover. I put my body through hell to get it in this shape. And Conseco knows what steroids can do to your body. Anyway, I'm out of here, but not before I let everyone know what happened."

Balarie watched the crowds move in closer. "Conseco's not on steroids."

"Oh really. Has no one ever wondered why he doesn't have a girlfriend? Yeah, steroids make you bulk up, but they leave your love life a total disaster. I may be leaving, but I think the media will love this story. Tell Conseco to check the papers in a day or two." He shoved his shoulder sideways as security walked in. "Don't worry guys. I'm leaving."

Balarie glanced at the people in the hallway. Word of this will get back to Tommy soon. Did she handle it correctly? And she knew better since Tommy had no erection dysfunctional type problems. At least the night they made love he didn't have any problems at all. She walked back in her office and shut the door.

She soon heard a knock on the door, as Olivia opened it to walk in. "I heard what happened. Mr. Conseco's not going to be happy with bad press."

"I can imagine."

"To him, image is everything. I'm sure he'll call a press meeting also to counter any accusations. He'll need everyone on the staff here to support him. He should be in the office in about an hour. He always likes to make a preemptive strike. Reports of this will go viral on the internet in no time."

"I'll be there."

"Good. And don't take it hard, it wasn't your fault, you inherited this problem."

###

Tommy rushed into his office to avoid any questions. Any attack on him or his company was personal. He had worked out with this model before, and they had talked about steroids. As tempted as he was, however, he never tried any. Proving it would take some time. While he would submit to testing for steroids, how could he prove he wasn't impotent?

He remembered a problem like this once before when a rumor had circulated that he was gay. He had to tread on it lightly since many of the models had special connections with the gay community.

Now, with this hitting him at the worst possible time, he had to move fast. With him racing off to Milan for several weeks, he needed to control any chance of the rumor spreading.

Olivia knocked as she entered his office. "I've worked on a press meeting like you asked for. I hope we can lay it as a special promotion for the new shooting assignment Balarie obtained for us with a short mention of the Milan fashion week as a wrap up. However, we both know the press will move the conversation to the accusation thrown at you earlier."

"No doubt. Who's following the conversation on the internet?"

"I have several girls working on it. We both know we need to kill this story before the tabloids get their hands on it. They would love it."

"Definitely."

"Okay, leave me alone for a while and let me know when everyone's here."

"Yes, sir. Also I've arranged for several of our best models to attend and to stand behind you."

The image flashed in his mind, and he frowned at the implications which would be seen as false. "No, I think it will be seen as a fake this time. Let us keep the top staff around me and I'll handle it from there."

"Very good. I'll arrange it for you."

The next two hours passed slowly. He planned his words carefully. Olivia finally buzzed him—it was showtime.

A presentation stand centered the room normally used to teach models how to walk a runway. Chairs were arranged to hold around thirty or forty people. He knew many reporters had busted their butts to get a chance to ask him questions. Covering a breaking scandal could always make their careers.

Many people working for him on the executive floor stood on his far right side.

Their numbers reinforced his confidence. He felt ready for anything as he took his place.

He started the meeting by highlighting what Conseco Modeling had in the works. It was a perfect pitch session he didn't want to waste. He pushed it as far as he could, but knew the press only had so much patience. He knew why they came. It was time to allow them to ask questions.

The first tall skinny girl to stand jumped immediately into it. "We all have heard rumors today and thought you might want to reply to them."

He remained motionless as he waited for her to clarify her question.

"You have a reputation for housing some very masculine, muscular, macho male models. We all know how much steroids are abused in the bodybuilding industry. So I'll ask it straight out, but in two questions. One, is this something you push your models into using and secondly, do you use steroids yourself?"

"The first question is easy to answer. We maintain a strict policy against drug usage of any kind. Our models are randomly checked. Not only do we check the male models for steroids, but the females are also monitored for drugs used to reduce their weight. We support a healthy lifestyle that we want out models to enjoy.

Another girl pressed forward. "You appear to be in good shape for a guy who is, how many years is it now?"

"For the record it's thirty nine and I do work out very often. I think it's important to stay in shape."

"And you've never used steroids or other muscle enhancers, even once?"

"I use only standard over the counter vitamins anyone can buy." He felt the assault on his person, but it had been done before and he assumed it would for the rest of his life.

The tall girl stepped forward, unrelenting in her efforts to nail a story. "You're often seen about town with your models nearby. I'll get right to the reason most people suspect you might be using steroids. The talk is you're impotent and it's caused by steroids. After all, how could a guy like you avoid the multitudes of beauties around you day after day?"

"I think I have made it clear on many occasions that my company has a policy of no intercompany affairs, and no sexual harassment is ever allowed or even the hint of such."

"Many companies have such rules on the job, but what about off the job?"

"I stay much too busy for a normal life."

"You recently had a male model leave your firm saying he knows you used steroids."

"Unfortunately we have many models leave for one reason or another. This is a competitive business. Some don't leave us feeling too happy about it."

Tommy glanced at Balarie taking this in. So far, no one had asked about her. He hoped she understood why he needed to defend his honor. He also hoped no one would direct questions at their newly formed relationship, which was still developing.

"I'm sure you know we'll be talking to him and others you work out with. You've had an amazing run as the most eligible bachelor in the city."

Tommy turned to Balarie, and focused all of his attention on her instead of the unruly crowd, and he knew it. "It has been a great run, but I guess all good things must end one day." A single

wink fetched immediate attention from the crowd. "I know you're all after a story. I suggest you wait for me in Italy, where I'll be attending fashion week."

Balarie still hadn't given him an answer, but he hoped he could convince her to, perhaps even now. Should he push?

Another older lady rose and yelled above the crowds. "I've been covering the fashion scene for more than a quarter of a century, and there's not much that escapes my attention. Even tango dances that I didn't get invited to this year, but I still managed to slip into." Her rough Brooklyn accent quieted the last members of the media. "I always thought one day, one girl would steal your heart. Some rules are meant to be broken." She turned to Balarie. "I assume that I'll be seeing you in Italy also."

###

Balarie watched the crowds shift their attention to her. This wasn't supposed to happen like this. She had leaned toward going, yes, but she wanted to talk to Tommy one more time. "Tommy has asked me to go with him." She shifted her focus back to a guy who offered her a gentle reassuring smile. How could she really say *no* to Tommy?

The older lady continued. "I've seen the photos of the two of you out on the town. You would think after twenty five years of covering this guy, I would get at least one good exclusive out of him."

If there was ever a time she needed to be rescued, it was now. She knew the questions would escalate. Still, her focus centered on Tommy. He deserved someone far better than her.

"We've only known each other for a short time."

The tall rude mouth girl pressed forward. "How do you feel about getting involved with a guy who might possibly be impotent?"

The night of sex with Tommy heated her thoughts, but her anger at this girl's insults melted her last ounce of resistance. "I hate to disappoint you, but I'm having Tommy's baby."

With the result totally anticipated, she prepared her eyes for the onslaught of flashes, and questions flying from all corners of the room. She held her hands in front of her and walked toward Tommy, who managed to maintain a slinky smile. "I think Tommy

answered a question earlier I hope you'll all take an advantage of. We'll be together in Milan during fashion week." She turned toward him and winked.

Chapter 24

With the last few days a blur, Balarie handled last-minutes details while experiencing the trauma in hiding from the media and paparazzi. While the yacht would depart tomorrow morning, Tommy had arranged for her to join him the night before on the boat. She felt nervous as she walked on board what would be her home for the next week and the gateway to her future.

The manager greeted her immediately. "It's so nice to have you on board, Ms. Danson. I look forward to this next week."

"I do also. The driver behind me is bringing my luggage. I didn't know exactly what to carry."

"Mr. Conseco's waiting for you on the top section. We'll take care of your luggage."

Climbing the stairways felt like climbing her way to heaven. She saw him standing in the front of the boat, patiently waiting on her with a brilliant smile. "Thanks for coming tonight, Balarie. This way we can outfox the media tomorrow morning. They will not realize we came a night earlier."

"What about the others?"

"I suspect the paparazzi will be waiting on us and allow them to pass, hoping not to spook us." He reached over and placed an arm around her. "This will also give us one night alone before the rest join us."

She relaxed slightly. "I like the way you think. They're bringing my luggage to . . . our room. Perhaps I should slip into something more relaxing or comfortable, as the case might be. What do you think?"

The lights inside his heart glowed through his iris, and the pupils expanded to their limit. "Are you sure? You know there's a rumor out there I'm impotent."

"I think I might be the only one qualified to dispel such slander. Still, a second trial by fire would be good. You know . . . just for verification." Balarie enjoyed the teasing, and especially his acceptance and encouragement to continue.

"I had to make a few changes to the master cabin on board since I last saw you." He glanced to his side, and in the direction of their cabin

"Oh really."

"Yes, I wanted it to generate a more of our feel than the old days of my taste, if that makes sense."

"Yes, I can see where I might need to make a few changes, you know, here and there." She wondered how much he would allow her to change his style. "Being a bachelor for a long time, I assume it will take a while for you to get used to having someone else around."

"I think I can adjust. I want to show you it first, and enjoy our first glass of champagne together before anyone else joins us. I have a bottle in our cabin."

"Well, one thing is for sure, you sure never beat around the bush, do you?"

He smiled, and radiated a deep inner personal connection which she could not avoid any longer as she leaned over and kissed him. The moment her lips touched his, she felt his arms around her pulling her closer, and uniting them in a bond that she knew she would love forever.

"I never do anything slow. I also never do anything without thinking through it fully. Shall we see which champagne is waiting for us?"

"I think champagne sounds like an excellent idea."

She wrapped her arm around his and walked along the hallway to the stairs. She knew they would be on the boat for a long time. What she didn't know was how he would act when the others arrived tomorrow.

He opened the door to their cabin and they walked in. The color scheme had changed—new paint. The bold red colors from before had disappeared and were replaced by subtle relaxing blues. The room smelled perfect, as roses on the center table added the perfect dash of color. And, of course, the champagne in the pail of ice looked so damn inviting.

Tommy motioned to the table. "I do have a special toast. So if you'll allow me." He reached for the bottle and examined it intensely. "I've managed to purchase one of the best from the champagne regions in France, and one which is usually all shipped to Russia. I think you'll like it." He proceeded to open the bottle.

"I'm sure I will." She enjoyed the rush of anticipation. "So . . . what is it that we will toast to tonight?"

He walked closer to her and removed a small box from his pocket. "I think this."

From the ring-sized box, she knew, or at least, thought she knew. "I . . . ."

Tommy opened the box for her, exposing a diamond larger than anything she had ever seen before. "I hope it fits, but if not we'll have it adjusted. I've never done this before, and I never plan on doing it again.”

Balarie studied the ring, but waited for words to materialize. Previous visions of this happening escaped her. Her focus shifted to him.

“I want you to marry me. I want you to be my wife, and to raise a family with. We can marry at sea, in Milan or have a major wedding back in the city. I don’t care where. I only care that you accept me for who I am, and not for who the public thinks I am.”

“I . . . don’t know what to say.”

“Perhaps I can help. I have one more thing I need to tell you.”

“Which is?”

“Balarie, I love you.”

Tears flooded her eyes. The thoughts of love entered her mind, words she didn’t know how to say until now. “Since I can call you Tommy, and since your mother is available, I think a wedding at sea would be perfect.”

Joy quickly flooded her expression. “Then, it’s a yes?”

“Yes, I love you too, and I do want to marry you.” She leaned forward and devoured his mouth, accepting a kiss she wanted to disappear inside of forever.

“I think I need to leave a note on the door for the crew not to disturb us until late in the morning. What do you think?" He reached for the menu card on the table and casually glanced at the list of breakfast items. "And one more question. How do you want your egg in the morning?"

Balarie focused on his eyes, which were as blue as the sea she hoped to see tomorrow before she so softly, but hopefully seductively whispered, "Fertilized."

THE END